THE WINNING EDGE SERIES

Dreams
of Gold

Published in Nashville, Tennessee, by Tommy Nelson™, a division of Thomas Nelson, Inc. Executive Editor: Laura Minchew; Managing Editor: Beverly Phillips. Book design by Kandi Shepherd.

Unless otherwise indicated, Scripture quotations are from the *International Children's Bible, New Century Version,* copyright © 1983, 1986, 1988 by Word Publishing.

Library of Congress Cataloging-in-Publication Data
Kirby, Lynn. 1956–
　　Dreams of Gold / by Lynn Kirby
　　　　p. cm.—(The winning edge series ; 3)
　　Summary: Jamie, a talented African-American skater with dreams of winning many titles, will do anything to be like the national champion Brianna Hill, but then she realizes that Christ is the only real role model.
　　ISBN 0-8499-5837-7
　　[1. Ice skating—Fiction. 2. Afro-Americans—Fiction.
　3. Christian life—Fiction.] I. Title. II. Series: Kirby, Lynn, 1956–
　Winning edge series ; 3.
　PZ7.K633523Dr 1998
　[Fic]—dc21

　　　　　　　　　　　　　　　　　　　　　　　　　98–18723
　　　　　　　　　　　　　　　　　　　　　　　　　　CIP
　　　　　　　　　　　　　　　　　　　　　　　　　　AC

Printed in the United States of America
99 00 01 02 DHC 9 8 7 6 5 4 3

BOOK THREE
THE
WINNING
EDGE
SERIES

Dreams of Gold

Lynn Kirby

Tommy
NELSON™

Thomas Nelson, Inc.
Nashville

For Amy, Audra, Daemey, Esther,
Megan, and Sarah,
who truly understand
what it means to be a champion.

Figure Skating Terms

Boards—The barrier around the ice surface is often referred to as "the boards."

Choreography—The arrangement of dance to music. In figure skating, it would be figure skating moves to music.

Crossovers—While going forward or backward, the skater crosses one foot over the other.

Edges—The skate blade has two sharp edges with a slight hollow in the middle. The edge on the outside of the foot is called the "outside edge." The edge on the inside of the foot is called the "inside edge."

Footwork—A series of turns, steps, and positions executed while moving across the ice.

Jumps

Axel—A jump that takes off from a forward outside edge. The skater makes one and a half turns in the air to land on a back outside edge of the opposite foot. A *Double Axel Jump* is the same as the axel, but the skater rotates two and a half times in the air. For a *Triple Axel,* the skater rotates three and a half times.

Ballet Jump—From a backward outside edge, the skater taps the ice behind with the toe pick, and springs into the air, turning forward. The jump appears as a simple, graceful leap, landing forward.

Bunny Hop—A beginner jump. The skater springs forward from one foot, touches down with the toe pick of the other foot, and lands on the original foot going forward.

Combination Jump—The skater performs two or more jumps without making a turn or step in between.

Flip Jump—From a back inside edge, the skater takes off by thrusting a toe pick into the ice behind her, vaults into the air where she makes a full turn, and lands on the back outside edge of the other foot. A *Double Flip Jump* is the same as the flip jump, but with two rotations. For a *Triple Flip,* the skater makes three rotations.

Loop Jump—The skater takes off from a back outside edge, makes a full turn in the air, and lands on the same back outside edge. A *Double Loop Jump* is the same as the loop jump, but the skater rotates two times. For a *Triple Loop Jump,* the skater completes three rotations.

Lutz Jump—Similar to the flip jump except the skater takes off from a back outside edge, thrusts a toe pick into the ice, makes a full turn in the air, and lands on the back outside edge of the other foot. Usually done in the corner. A *Double Lutz Jump* is the same as the lutz jump, but with two rotations. A *Triple Lutz Jump* is the same as the lutz jump, but the skater makes three full rotations.

Salchow Jump—The skater takes off from a back inside edge, makes a full turn in the air, and lands on the back outside edge of the other foot. A *Double Salchow* is the same as the salchow, but the skater makes two full rotations. For a *Triple Salchow,* the skater makes three rotations.

Toe Loop Jump—The skater takes off from a back out-side edge assisted by a toe pick thrust, makes a full turn in the air, and lands on the back outside edge of the same foot. A *Double Toe Loop* is the same as the toe loop jump, but with two rotations. For a *Triple Toe Loop,* the skater makes three full rotations.

Waltz Jump—The skater takes off from a forward out-side edge, makes a half turn, and lands on the back outside edge of the other foot.

Moves in the Field—Figure skaters must pass a series of tests in order to advance to each competitive level. These tests consist of stroking, edges, and turns skated in prescribed patterns. Sometimes referred to as Field Moves.

Spins

Camel Spin—A spin in an arabesque position.

Combination Spin—The skater changes from one position to another while continuing to spin.

Flying Camel—A flying spin. The skater jumps from a forward outside edge and lands in a camel position rotating on the backward outside edge of the opposite foot.

Layback Spin—A spin that is completed with the skater's head and shoulders leaning backward with the free leg bent behind in an "attitude" position.

One-foot Spin—An upright spin on one foot.

Sit Spin—A spin performed in a "sitting" position, on a bent knee with the free leg extended in front.

Two-foot Spin—The first spin a skater learns. The skater uses both feet.

Shoot-the-duck—One leg is extended in front while the skater glides on a deeply bent knee.

Skate Guards—Rubber protectors worn over skating blades when walking off ice. Also called blade guards.

Spiral—The skater glides down the ice on one foot with the free leg extended high in back.

Spread Eagle—The skater glides on two feet with toes pointed outward.

Stroking—Pushing with one foot, then the other, to glide across the ice.

Three-turn—A turn on one foot from forward to backward or backward to forward. Traces a "3" on the ice.

Toe Picks—The sharp teeth on the front of the figure skating blade. Used to assist in turns, jumps, and spins.

Zamboni—The large machine used to make the ice surface smooth.

One

Jamie Summers shivered in the cool spring breeze as she followed her coach into the ice skating rink. It was early April, and Jamie was in Nashville to compete against some of the best young skaters in the country at the Music City Trophy Competition. Jamie felt that just to be invited to compete was a real honor.

If only Mom had been able to come, she thought regretfully.

Always before Jamie's mother, an attorney for a large corporation, managed to attend Jamie's competitions. However, since Jamie and her mother had moved from Atlanta, Georgia, to the small town of Walton just outside of Dallas, Texas, she hadn't seen her mother as much as she wanted.

I wish she hadn't taken that stupid promotion. Then we'd still be in Atlanta, Jamie thought.

Her coach, Elena Grischenko, gently guided her into the rink. As they looked around her coach said, "It is a good rink, Jamie."

Although Coach Grischenko was nice, Jamie had only been taking lessons with her for a couple of months and was still a little in awe of the well-known Ukrainian coach. With her chin-length dark blond hair and piercing blue eyes, Coach Grischenko demanded perfection from her students.

Jamie went through her stretching routine and then quickly laced up her skates. Coach Grischenko took her place at the side of the rink, watching intently while Jamie began warming up.

Jamie was a very talented skater and one of the few African-American girls within the higher ranks of competitive figure skating. Almost thirteen, she had been skating since she was three. Last fall, she had won the novice-level championship for her region, which qualified her to compete at the larger sectional championships. The top skaters at sectionals go on to compete at nationals, but Jamie had skated badly and only placed fifth. Still, she had earned an invitation to this special competition.

Even though this was only a practice session, Jamie felt a little nervous. She knew that judges often watched the practice sessions. She really wanted to win this competition, or at least win a medal. But it would be tough. Two of the best young skaters in the country were competing: Tamara Vasiliev and Kayla Anderson.

Jamie knew she had a chance, but to win she would have to skate perfectly.

The competition consisted of two programs: a short technical program in which certain jumps and spins were required, and an artistic program. Jamie had competed in the short program the day before, and she was pleased to be in third place. Still, she knew she could have skated better.

For the first time, Jamie had three triple jumps in her program. She had never included more than one triple jump before, but Coach Grischenko felt that she would need more than one triple to win. Could she really land three?

During the practice session, Jamie landed the first triple salchow* she tried, and it only took two tries to get the triple toe loop*. The triple flip* was the most difficult move in her program, and she hadn't been working on it very long. Skating forward, she made a three-turn* onto the inside edge* of her left foot, jabbed her right toe pick* into the ice behind her, and vaulted into the air with all her strength. Once, twice, three times she rotated in the air and landed on the back outside edge of her right blade. But she was leaning a little too far forward when she came down and touched her right hand to the ice before she regained her balance.

Coach Grischenko gave her some instructions, and Jamie gave the triple flip another try—and another.

---

*An asterisk in the text indicates a figure skating term that is in the list of definitions on pages v-viii.

Every time she attempted the jump, it was worse than before, until finally the coach told her to stop.

Discouraged, Jamie got off the ice. She knew she needed to really impress the judges if she wanted to win this competition. Tamara Vasiliev, the novice national champion, was in first place after the short program. Jamie knew that Tamara had three triple jumps in her artistic long program, including the difficult triple lutz*. Although Jamie had occasionally worked on the triple lutz, she had never successfully landed it. She wasn't alone. Very few novice-level competitors, or even junior competitors, could perform the difficult jump.

Tamara was just getting on the ice for her practice session, and Jamie watched for a few minutes before she took off her skates. Like Jamie, Tamara was twelve years old, but she was very small for her age. Her short light brown hair gently bounced as she flew over the ice like a little bird. Because she was so tiny, her jumps were high and she could rotate very fast.

Jamie watched enviously, wishing she could jump like this tiny girl. Her own body was slim and athletic, but she was taller and more muscular than Tamara. Jamie wondered if it were really possible to beat her. Tamara was so good!

✱ ✱ ✱ ✱ ✱

After eating supper in the hotel dining room, Coach Grischenko and Jamie returned to their hotel room. "I have an important meeting downstairs," the coach told Jamie. "Will you be okay here?"

4

"Sure," said Jamie. "There's a movie on I can watch."

Coach Grischenko nodded. "Keep the door locked. Do not open it for anyone but me. I will be back in about an hour."

Jamie was secretly relieved to have her stern coach gone for a while. Now she could relax. However, Coach Grischenko had only been gone a few minutes when Jamie began to feel lonely.

She pulled out the new Bible her mother had given to her as a special gift for her first time at a competition by herself. "I'm sorry I can't be with you," her mother had said, "but God is always there." Jamie ran her hands over its raspberry leather cover.

A year ago Jamie had asked Jesus to be her Savior, and she was still learning about what that meant. She had heard someone say that she should read the Bible every day. She decided now was a good time to start. Jamie sat down and began reading. She didn't understand everything, but somehow reading God's Word made her feel less lonely.

While putting the Bible safely back in her suitcase, she noticed the package from her friends in Walton. Jamie took out the brown paper package and stared at it longingly. Her friends had instructed her to wait until the next morning to open it, but Jamie wanted to open it now. She was sure her friends wouldn't mind.

Jamie sat down on one of the beds and pulled off the brown paper to find two smaller packages inside—one wrapped in blue paper with white stars and another wrapped in newspaper comics. Jamie opened the star package first. Inside was a small teddy bear wearing skates and with a tiny medal hanging around its neck. A note tied to it read "Always a Winner!" and was signed by Amy, Kristen, Shannon, and Tiffany.

Jamie thought about her new friends. She had been surprised to find talented skaters like Kristen Grant and Amy Pederson in such a small town as Walton. And Shannon Roberts, whom Jamie found truly amazing. Shannon had started skating only the fall before, along with her six-year-old sister, Tiffany, and she was quickly becoming quite good. Maybe it was all those years of ballet. Kristen, Amy, and Shannon had all turned thirteen. Like Jamie, they were in the seventh grade. Jamie had only been in town a few weeks when the girls admired her skating and introduced themselves.

I wish Amy and Kristen could have come to this competition, thought Jamie as she hugged the little bear to herself. But this was a special competition to which only regional champions had received invitations. And Jamie was the only one of her coach's students who had been invited this year.

Gently putting the bear down, Jamie picked up the package wrapped in comics. It had to be from Kevin, Kristen's twin brother. Curious, she pulled open the wrappings, wondering what Kevin might have sent. Inside were a couple of candy bars and a note that read: "These are not for you. Give them to your toughest competitor right before the competition. She'll overdose on sugar and skate badly!" Jamie laughed—Kevin was such a practical joker. She'd save the candy bars to eat *after* the competition! The card flipped off and landed facedown on the bed. On the back it read: "I bet you opened this before we told you to!" Of course, he'd been right.

Jamie looked at her alarm clock. Coach Grischenko had already been gone longer than she had intended. She pulled out her phone card. Her mother had called earlier that afternoon, but she had given Jamie permission to use the card to call one of her friends. She decided to call Kristen. She wanted to let Kevin and Kristen know how much she appreciated the gifts. And Kristen was dependable—she'd remember to tell the others Jamie called.

Jamie dialed Kristen's number, hoping she was home. "Hello?"

"Kristen, it's Jamie!"

"Jamie! Wait! I'll put on the speakerphone. Amy and Shannon are here!"

Jamie waited while Kristen switched on the speakerphone. "Hi, Jamie!" shouted the girls on the other end of the line.

"Hey, this is great!" said Jamie. "I can talk to all of you. Thanks for the gifts!"

"Kevin was right, you opened them early!" yelled Amy.

"Yeah. I couldn't wait. I *love* the teddy bear! I'm going to take him with me when I compete tomorrow! Oh! And tell Kevin thanks for the candy bars!"

Kristen laughed. "He's so silly!"

"Hey, have you already skated the short program?" shouted Amy.

"Yesterday," answered Jamie. "I'm in third place. Mainly because I messed up my double lutz*."

"Third place! That's great!" said Shannon.

"Who's in first and second?" asked Kristen.

"Tamara Vasiliev is in first," said Jamie. "You should see her. She's real tiny and really, really good."

"How old is she?" asked Shannon.

"Twelve. Kayla Anderson is in second," said Jamie.

"I bet you'll beat them both in the artistic program," said Shannon confidently.

"I don't know," said Jamie doubtfully. "Coach Grischenko wants me to put a triple flip in my program, but I can't seem to land it."

"Can you win without it?" asked Kristen.

Jamie sighed. "No. Tamara and Kayla both have three triple jumps in their programs."

"I've seen you land lots of triple flips," encouraged Amy. "You can do it!"

"I couldn't do one today," said Jamie.

"We'll be praying for you," said Kristen. "I wish we could be there to cheer you on."

"Me, too," admitted Jamie. "It's kind of lonely here with just Coach Grischenko. I think she's allergic to fun!"

"I don't think she's ever heard of the word!" said Amy, then she laughed. Both Kristen and Amy were also students of Coach Grischenko. "If we were there, you'd be having a blast."

"We'll make up for it when you get home," said Shannon. "We're going to—"

"Shhh!" interrupted Amy.

"Oh, I forgot!" said Shannon. "Never mind."

"What?" demanded Jamie. "Don't keep me in suspense!"

"Well," said Kristen, "we have plans for a celebration when you get home, but it was supposed to be a surprise."

"Just skate your best tomorrow," said Shannon. "Then we can *really* celebrate."

"I'll try," said Jamie. "I think I hear Coach Grischenko at the door. I'd better hang up."

"Good luck!" called out Kristen, Shannon, and Amy.

Jamie wished her friends were there with her. Suddenly, she felt lonelier than ever.

❄ ❄ ❄ ❄ ❄

Jamie tried to ignore the noise in the arena. She only had a few minutes on the ice to warm up, and she needed to focus on preparing for her program.

Focus, focus! she repeated to herself. Jamie was determined to land that triple flip in her program. After warming up on some of her other moves, she gave it a try. The first two times she fell. Finally, she landed on one foot, but, just like the day before, she was leaning a little too far forward when she came down and touched her right hand to the ice before she regained her balance. It wasn't her best triple flip, but at least she had landed it.

Jamie looked over to her coach for instruction, but Coach Grischenko merely nodded and motioned for her to continue with her warmup.

There was so much to think about! Jamie struggled to keep her mind on her own skating while avoiding the other skaters on the ice. Although there were only five other girls in the warmup, they were all skating at such high speeds that it wasn't easy to stay out of their way. Several times Jamie had to skid to a stop to avoid a collision.

She was relieved when the warmup was over. She stepped off the ice and slipped on her skate guards* before following her coach to a waiting area.

Waiting for her turn to skate was nearly unbearable. Coach Grischenko talked to her about her program, giving her last-minute instructions, but Jamie hardly heard her. She was too nervous.

"Jamie, are you listening?" asked Coach Grischenko, frowning.

"Uh, yes, ma'am," Jamie said, startled back to reality.

"This is an important competition," said her coach, her Ukrainian accent punctuating her words. "Think very hard." She tapped Jamie's head. "If you win, it will be from here."

Jamie listened impatiently. This was her first major competition with Coach Grischenko, and the best advice she had given her was to "think hard." Jamie missed her old coach from Atlanta, Emily Cassanbeck. Emily always knew that humor was how to boost

Jamie's confidence before she competed. So, Emily used to crack jokes and make Jamie laugh while she waited for her turn to skate. She wished Emily were here now.

Tamara and Kayla both skated before Jamie, but she knew it wasn't a good idea to watch them perform. If they skated well, she would be nervous because she would feel she had no chance to win. If they skated badly, she would worry that she might skate badly as well. It was best to focus on being ready for her own program instead of thinking about the other skaters. Jamie had brought her portable disc player; she put in her favorite CD and listened with earplugs, hoping to drown out everything.

Still, it was impossible not to know what was going on. Kayla came off the ice in tears after her program. Jamie wondered what had happened. However, Tamara's face showed no emotion after she skated, so Jamie couldn't tell how well Tamara had performed. *It doesn't really matter,* she told herself, *I'll have to skate my best if I'm going to have any chance of winning.*

At last it was time for Jamie to skate. She stepped on the ice, looked back for a nod of encouragement from her coach, and skated to her starting position. The music of Hungarian Rhapsody no. 2 filled the arena. Jamie's dark eyes showed her determination to succeed.

Jamie was a little nervous at first, and she almost tripped as she started the short footwork* pattern at the beginning of her program. However, she soon recovered her composure and focused her energy on skating well.

Double lutz–double loop combination jump*. Double axel*. Flying camel* into a grab-foot spin, a move in which Jamie grabbed her skate blade as she spun. Triple toe loop. Footwork. Triple salchow. One by one Jamie completed every move in her program. She knew she was skating well.

When it was time for the triple flip jump*, Jamie wavered just a little. Could she do it? But she knew if she wanted to win, she needed another triple jump.

She blocked out everything and set up the jump. Posture, speed, arm position—everything had to be just right. She thrust her right toe pick into the ice behind her and leaped into the air, pulling her arms in tightly. But she knew immediately that something was not right. She made three full rotations before she crashed hard into the ice.

There was no time to think about the fall. Jamie knew she had to quickly scramble back to her feet and focus on the remaining portion of her program. One jump might not matter.

Jamie finished her program. As she stepped off the ice she considered the missed jump. Although she had skated well, she was sure there was no way she could win this competition unless the others had missed their jumps, and that was unlikely.

Coach Grischenko seemed pleased, but all she said was "You skated well." And Jamie could never quite tell by the tight-lipped smile on her coach's face whether she was happy or unhappy with a performance.

Jamie hated waiting for the results. Her coach asked her if she wanted something to eat. Jamie had eaten nothing since breakfast, but she was too nervous to be hungry. She had really wanted to win this competition. Jamie sat down and tried to watch the other skaters, but all she could think about was that she hadn't landed the triple flip jump.

"Jamie?" Coach Grischenko was in front of her, holding a sheet of paper. Jamie looked up, anxious to know the results but afraid at the same time. The coach's face was nearly expressionless, except for the twinkle in her eye.

"Congratulations, Jamie, you have first place!"

Jamie gasped. "But I missed my triple flip!"

The coach shrugged. "Tamara only landed one of her triples—she fell on the others."

"I can't wait to tell my mom! She made me promise to call her as soon as I found out how I did!"

Coach Grischenko handed her a cell phone.

Jamie excitedly punched in her mother's direct office number. She could hardly believe it. She had beaten the national novice champion—even though she had fallen!

As soon as her mother answered, Jamie yelled, "Mom! I won!"

Two

"Surprise!" Jamie's mom and her friends were waiting in the airport to greet Jamie and Coach Grischenko as they stepped off the plane. Kristen and her twin brother, Kevin, held a big sign saying: "Welcome back, Jamie Summers: Champion Figure Skater!" It never failed to amaze Jamie how much the two looked alike. Standing next to Kristen was Amy, a slender girl with pale blond hair. Shannon, a petite girl with Asian features, had also come, along with her little sister, Tiffany. Mrs. Grant, Kristen and Kevin's mother, accompanied the group.

People in the lobby were watching curiously as Tiffany filled Jamie's arms with flowers. Jamie felt a little embarrassed by all the attention. Still, it was nice to know her friends cared enough to come to meet her.

Jamie's mother gave her a big hug. "I'm so proud of you, Jamie!" she said.

"Thanks, Mom! It's really cool that all of you came

to see me," Jamie said. She turned to her mother. "When we get home I'll show you my medal."

"That will have to be tonight, Jamie. Mrs. Grant is going to take you home. I've got a meeting in Dallas."

Jamie's face fell. She loved being with her friends, but she was anxious to tell her mother all about the competition. "Do you really have to go?"

"I'm sorry, Jamie," said her mother sadly. "I tried to change the meeting, but at least I got it postponed. I wanted to be here to greet you." She gave Jamie another hug, and turned to Coach Grischenko.

"Thank you for taking Jamie to the competition," she said. "And, Elaine, thank you for taking Jamie home. Now, I've got to run." She turned and briskly walked away.

Mrs. Grant put her arm around Jamie's shoulders and gave her a hug. "I know you are disappointed. But it took a lot of work for your mother to even meet us here. And, she did arrange for all of us to be here."

Mrs. Grant turned to Coach Grischenko. "I believe the baggage claim is this way." As the two women walked toward the baggage claim, Jamie's friends surrounded her.

"Were you surprised?" asked Shannon, her dark eyes sparkling.

"Definitely," said Jamie.

"What a week. It's great to have you back," said Amy. "Things haven't been the same without you!"

"Yeah," said Kevin, "they have to get *me* to help them with their jumps."

Amy, Shannon, and Kristen cried together, "Did not!"

Kevin shook his head in disbelief. "Can you believe that? They don't even appreciate all the help I've given them." He gave his sister's braided hair a quick tug.

"Mom, make Kevin behave!" protested Kristen.

Mrs. Grant shot both Kevin and Kristen a warning look. Then she turned to Jamie. "Jamie, grab your bags. Kevin, please get Coach Grischenko's luggage."

When everything had been collected, Mrs. Grant turned to Coach Grischenko. "I'll be glad to give you a ride."

"Thank you, but it is not necessary," said the coach. "I have my car. We did not expect this surprise party." She looked at Jamie and actually smiled. "You enjoy your friends, and I will see you tomorrow morning, yes?"

Jamie nodded a bit reluctantly, as the coach said her good-byes to everyone. *Emily would have insisted I take a day off after a competition,* Jamie thought.

❄ ❄ ❄ ❄ ❄

It was a long drive home from the airport, but there was a lot to talk about.

"Jamie, guess what Amy did?" asked Tiffany.

"Tiff, don't tell on me!" complained Amy.

Jamie was curious now. "What?"

"Amy is going to be on TV," said Tiffany, giggling.

"You're going to be on TV?" asked Jamie. She looked at Amy for an explanation.

"Don't ask!" moaned Amy.

"Some TV reporters came to the rink this morning," said Kristen. "I think they're doing a story on the rink."

"And she crashed!" said Tiffany, barely able to get the words out through her laughter.

"Tiff!" yelled Amy. "It was so stupid. I walked around to get on TV and—"

"You got on TV okay!" exclaimed Tiffany.

". . . and right in front of the cameras I stepped on the ice with my skate guards on!"

"We heard a crash and there was Amy, sprawled over the ice!" said Shannon.

Amy's pale face turned red. "I hope they don't show *that* on the news!"

"I hope they do. I called all the guys and told them to watch," Kevin said.

"You didn't!" yelled Amy.

"Nah, but I could have," Kevin said, and then he turned his attention to Jamie. "Hey, we brought you some goodies. Why don't you open them?" Kevin held up a gift bag hopefully.

Well aware of Kevin's antics, Jamie eyed the bag suspiciously.

Kristen laughed. "It really is food. He's just hungry."

"It's cookies," said Amy. "We made them for you last night."

"Yeah, we were so excited you won that competition!" said Shannon. "That is *so* cool!"

"Thanks, guys," said Jamie, taking the bag Kevin offered. She was enjoying the attention from her friends. "I don't know what to say."

"Say you'll come to a celebration party on Saturday," said Kristen.

"Sure, if it's okay with my mom," said Jamie.

"It's okay with her. My mom asked her already," said Kristen.

"We're going to the Tropical Cafe at the West End Plaza Mall for lunch," said Amy. "Isn't that cool?"

Jamie hadn't been to the new mall or the Tropical Cafe. "Uh, I guess so."

Amy looked disappointed. "Would you like to do something else? After all, this party's for you."

"No," said Jamie. "It'll be fun. I mean, whatever you guys want to do is fine with me."

"Can I come, too?" begged Tiffany.

"You're going to the zoo." Shannon looked at her sister in disbelief. "How many times do I have to remind you?"

"Oh, yeah. I could do both!"

Shannon rolled her eyes. Tiffany was adorable, but a nuisance at times.

Kristen turned to Jamie. "Mom will pick you up at eleven on Saturday morning."

❋ ❋ ❋ ❋ ❋

It wasn't easy getting up early for skating practice the next morning. Jamie punched the button on the alarm clock and rolled out of bed, but she wasn't happy about it. After years of getting up in time for early morning practices, she felt she occasionally deserved a break. *Emily would have given me the day off,* she thought. *I don't know why Coach Grischenko wants me to be there this morning.*

It wasn't much easier when she arrived at the rink. Jamie had hoped for some words of praise from her coach after winning such an important competition. However, Coach Grischenko had apparently forgotten all about Jamie's recent victory.

"Today we will work on 'moves in the field'* for the junior level test," announced the coach at the beginning of the lesson.

Jamie groaned. She knew that in order to move up to the next competitive level she would have to take two tests. The first was a test of moves in the field, consisting of footwork and turns skated in specific patterns around the ice surface. The second was a freestyle test on jumps and spins.

Jamie knew that practicing and passing these tests improved her skating, but she didn't enjoy doing it. Emily, her coach in Atlanta, had always let her work on what she enjoyed most—jumps and spins.

"You should have taken this test by now. Why have you not passed this test?" asked Coach Grischenko.

"I was busy getting ready for the sectional competition last fall," Jamie explained with just a hint of pride in her voice. After all, it was an honor to qualify for sectionals. "I didn't have time to work on field moves."

Coach Grischenko looked at her disapprovingly, seemingly unimpressed by Jamie's recent achievements. "Then we must begin right away."

For the next half-hour Jamie and her coach worked on the "moves" test. It was a very frustrating lesson for Jamie. It seemed nothing she did pleased her coach. As hard as she tried, she simply could not do the required patterns for the junior test.

"You must practice these moves every day," said the coach sternly.

Jamie thought she had never felt so discouraged. *Why didn't her coach recognize her abilities?* After all, she had just won an important competition. She had beaten Tamara Vasiliev, the national novice champion!

I miss Emily, thought Jamie irritably. *She believed in me. Coach Grischenko just doesn't know what I can do.* Jamie was so annoyed she hardly noticed when it was time to go. Suddenly, she looked around and found that she was alone. Everyone else had already gotten off the ice, and the big Zamboni* machine was being driven out onto the ice surface.

Jamie hurried into the lobby, where her friends were already getting ready to leave. Kevin was hanging around the video games with his new friend, Manuel, a thirteen-year-old figure skater who had recently begun skating at the Ice Palace. Manuel used to play hockey, but had switched to figure skating. After only a couple of years, he was already a very good skater.

"We thought you were going to skate all day!" said Amy.

Jamie sat down and quickly began unlacing her skates. "I guess it wouldn't be a bad idea. Coach Grischenko wants me to move up to the next level."

"Wow!" said Shannon, obviously impressed. Shannon had only been skating a few months, but she was already entering competitions. Her parents had recently

20

allowed her to begin practicing in the mornings along with the other girls.

Jamie sighed. "Yeah, she wants me to work really hard on my field moves so I can take the skating test for the junior level."

Amy looked a little envious. "You're way ahead of us already!"

"I just wish we didn't have to test moves in the field," complained Jamie. "They're boring!"

"I don't think so," said Kristen. "I like doing field moves."

Amy grinned at Jamie. "Yeah. She likes math word problems, too!"

Kristen shrugged. "Well—"

The other girls laughed. Nobody else was as disciplined as Kristen.

"Anyway," continued Jamie, "I guess I'll be competing at the junior level soon."

"Oh no!" said Kevin, as he grabbed his skate bag on the way to the door. "You know what that means!"

"What?" asked Kristen.

"She'll *really* think she owns the ice!" he said with a grin.

Her friends just laughed. They picked up their things and headed to the door. But Jamie wondered if they were just teasing or if that was what they really thought of her.

❈ ❈ ❈ ❈ ❈

An hour later Jamie arrived at Westbridge Academy for her first class. She sometimes wished she could go to public school with her friends, but then she would not be allowed the flexibility to attend so many competitions.

Jamie yawned while her homeroom teacher, Mrs. Davidson, took the roll. *I wish Mom would have let me skip school today,* she thought.

"Where have you been?" whispered Heather, who sat at the desk next to Jamie. Heather was very quiet, with curly red hair and freckles, but she was the only student in the private school who had tried to make friends with Jamie—outside of her skating friends.

"I've been to a competition in Nashville," said Jamie. "I got first place!"

"Cool!" said Heather. "You're so lucky!"

Westbridge was very different from Brookfield School, her old school in Atlanta. Brookfield was a school for gifted children involved in theater or sports. There every student worked at his or her own pace, with the teachers functioning as tutors. Jamie missed her teachers and friends at Brookfield. More and more she wished her mother hadn't taken that promotion.

❄ ❄ ❄ ❄ ❄

"Welcome back, Jamie," said Mrs. Wise, Jamie's social studies teacher. She was a popular teacher. "Would you like to tell us about your competition?"

Jamie looked around embarrassed as several of the other students stared curiously at her. Jamie had only attended the school for a couple of months. Since she left early every day, she hadn't had time to get to know the other students.

Self-consciously, she cleared her throat. "Um. It was an ice skating competition in Nashville. I took first place."

"Wow!" murmured some of the students, and there was a new look of respect on their faces.

"Was it hard?" someone asked.

"That one was. I had to earn the right to compete," Jamie said.

"Congratulations, Jamie! How exciting!" said Mrs. Wise.

"How long have you been ice skating?" someone yelled.

"Since I was three," said Jamie.

"Do you have to practice a lot?" someone else asked.

"I guess. I've done it so long. I practice before I come to school, and then I leave right after school to practice until dinner."

"Jamie, I think you should be very proud of yourself," her teacher said. "Students, you may discuss this with Jamie after class. Now, let's open our books . . ."

It was satisfying to hear the words of praise from her teacher and see the respect on the faces of the kids at school, especially after her lesson with Coach Grischenko that morning. Jamie felt good about her skating. It was nice to be recognized for her talent and hard work.

Jamie's next class was English. Miss Meyers, an attractive young woman with dark hair and eyes, was a very demanding teacher. As soon as Jamie took her seat, Miss Meyers asked for the book report assigned for last week.

Jamie gulped. She had completely forgotten about the report; she hadn't even read the book yet! At Brookfield

Jamie had always been given extra time to finish her assignments when she traveled to a competition.

"I'm sorry, Miss Meyers," she apologized. "I was so busy with the competition I didn't have time to finish the assignment. May I hand it in on Friday?"

Miss Meyers looked at her disapprovingly. "You have already had extra time. The other students handed in their reports *last* Friday."

Jamie didn't know what to say. She waited for Miss Meyers to tell her what she should do.

"I am sending a note home to your mother," said the teacher, "and a copy of the school policies. You may have two more days to finish the assignment, but it will cost you one grade level. The highest you can get now is a B. However, this is the last time I will accept a late assignment from you. Is that clear?"

"Yes, ma'am." Jamie swallowed hard. *Her teachers in Atlanta would never have made such a big deal about a little old book report. After all, skaters just don't need to know all this stuff.*

❄ ❄ ❄ ❄ ❄

"Mom, where's the pencil sharpener?" yelled Jamie from her room. After bringing home that note, she figured it would look better to her mom if she was doing her homework instead of spending time on the computer—like she normally did.

"Maybe Mrs. Wells put it in the desk drawer, or try the box of school supplies," called her mother from the kitchen. Mrs. Wells, the housekeeper, had already gone home for the day.

Jamie looked in the box labeled school supplies, but the pencil sharpener was not there. They'd been in Walton for more than two months, and her mother still hadn't found the time to finish unpacking. Annoyed, she thought, *If Mom would come home earlier she'd have everything in its place. And, what help is Mrs. Wells? She doesn't know where we want our stuff.*

Jamie couldn't do her math homework without sharpening her pencil, so she searched through every drawer and box in the house. Finally, in desperation, she sat down at the desk in her room to do the homework with an ink pen. But when she opened her desk drawer, there was the pencil sharpener!

Amazing! thought Jamie. *It was actually where it was supposed to be!*

Just then she heard the microwave "ping" and her mother yelled, "Ready to eat?"

Jamie's mom had brought home takeout for supper again. Tonight it was Chinese. Jamie missed her mother coming home and the two of them preparing something for dinner.

Things had been so different since they had moved to Walton. Her mother was rarely home, and she had hired Mrs. Wells to take care of their new townhouse and chauffeur Jamie to school and skating practice. Last week, she discussed adding cooking to Mrs. Wells's list of duties.

Jamie went into the kitchen, and there was her mother scooping rice onto their plates. Her mother was tall with very short black hair. She was still wearing the suit she'd worn to the office that day. She'd only had time to take off her shoes.

Jamie's parents had divorced when she was two. Lately, she had found herself wishing her dad lived with them—or at least nearby. *Maybe at least one of them could go with me to competitions.*

Jamie's mother looked up. "How was skating today?" she asked.

"Oh, fine. My coach wants me to get ready to take the next skating test."

Mrs. Summers nodded absently. "By the way, I heard about a good piano teacher for you. I'll try to give her a call this week."

Jamie made a face. "Do I have to take piano again?"

Her mother looked up. "Musical training is very important."

"But piano takes so much time," protested Jamie. "And I'm already so busy with skating. Besides, I'd rather play saxophone!"

"Maybe later. For now, it's piano," said Mrs. Summers. "How was school today?"

"Okay."

"Did anyone ask about the competition?"

"One of my teachers. And then the whole class was interested in ice skating." Jamie hesitated a moment. "After class, I even met some more of the students."

"That's wonderful, dear. Did anything else happen?"

Trying to sound unconcerned, Jamie added, "Oh, Miss Meyers sent a note home for you."

Unfortunately, that got her mother's attention. "Where is it?"

"I'll get it." Jamie went to her book bag and handed her mother the sealed note. She wished she had been able to read it first.

Mrs. Summers read the note soberly. "Jamie, do you know what this note is about?"

"Sort of."

Her mother folded the note and looked at her thoughtfully. "I know there have been a lot of changes for you in the last couple of months, but I expect you to keep up with your schoolwork. I'm very disappointed that you haven't turned in your homework assignments on time."

"But, Mom!" protested Jamie. "The teachers here give me tons of work, even when I have a big competition! I hate it. I wish we'd never left Atlanta."

"Jamie, I expected you to turn in your homework in Atlanta, too," her mother said.

"But it was different. They gave me more time," Jamie said.

"How long did you know about this assignment?"

"Um, four weeks," Jamie said quietly.

"Miss Meyers is right. You had plenty of time to finish this assignment before you went to the competition. Did she give you an extra week?"

"Yes."

"Jamie, we've had this conversation before. Your skating is important, but not as important as your education. I expect you to get your homework in on time."

There was silence in the kitchen as Jamie's mother put the plates on the table and poured them both some iced tea.

Finally, Jamie said, "I hate it here! You didn't think of me. You just wanted to move."

"That's enough, Jamie. You know one of the reasons I chose *this* transfer was so you could work with Coach Grischenko."

Jamie sat down at the table and poked her fork at her meal. She mumbled, "Coach Grischenko isn't as good a coach as Emily!"

Her mother stared at her. "Jamie, it takes time to make adjustments. And Coach Grischenko is very highly recommended. Emily was thrilled you would have the chance to work with her."

Jamie didn't say anything more. She knew she was already in trouble because of Miss Meyers's note.

Three

The West End Plaza Mall had opened some time ago, but Jamie had never been there. When her friends arranged a celebration at the Tropical Cafe there, she wondered what could be so special about a mall. Now she understood.

The doors slid open electronically and a voice greeted the group to the West End Plaza Mall. Once inside, Jamie gazed in amazement at the marble corridors and tropical plants. The effect was that of a tropical paradise, with stores selling everything imaginable. Mounted along the walkways every one hundred yards or so was a video monitor blaring out music videos. The whole place was noisy and busy, but very exciting.

"This is really cool!" said Jamie. Her friends grinned at one another, satisfied that Jamie seemed impressed.

"Can we shop by ourselves?" begged Kristen.

Mrs. Grant nodded yes. "As long as you stay in this

wing of the mall. I've got some shopping I need to do."
She looked at her watch. "I'll meet you right here in
ninety minutes."

"This mall has got some awesome video games!"
said Kevin, who had brought along Manuel.

"You kids stay in this part of the mall," warned Mrs.
Grant. "We'll meet at the cafe at one o'clock."

At that the two boys immediately departed for the
nearby video game room; the girls went the opposite
direction.

"Let's go to the music store," said Amy. "It's huge!"

"Okay," agreed Kristen. "I want to look for some
new piano music."

"You have to take piano?" asked Jamie.

"Yeah," said Kristen. "I really like it."

"I don't," said Jamie. "I *really* want to play the
saxophone."

The music store had almost every type of music
imaginable. Jamie headed straight for the gospel section
to look for her favorite Christian rap group.

Next, the girls all went to check out the accessory
store and a fashion boutique before finally going into
the bookstore.

Jamie headed for the science and technology section.
"I'm going to astronomy and computers," she said.

Amy frowned. "Boring!" she said. "I'm going to look
for books on skating."

"I'm with Amy," Shannon said as she scanned a display. Before Jamie was very far away she heard Shannon

yell, "Hey, look! There's that new book about Brianna Hill!" Shannon walked over to pick up the book. The other girls quickly joined her.

All three girls crowded around Shannon for a closer look.

"She's one of my favorite skaters," said Shannon.

Jamie picked up another copy and began flipping through the book. Brianna Hill, an African-American skater, had recently won the world championship. She was known for her triple axel*, an extremely difficult jump that few women in the world are able to do.

Shannon sighed as she looked at a picture of Brianna landing a jump. "I wish I could be like her!"

Amy nodded. "Yeah. She makes all those jumps look so easy."

"Well, after all, she's been skating all her life!" put in Kristen.

"Just like Jamie!" Amy laughed. "Hey!" She looked at the picture closely. "Jamie even *looks* kind of like her."

Jamie smiled. "I've just got to have this book." She opened her purse and began counting her money. "Just enough," she said.

"I think Coach Barnes knows her," said Kristen. "She once said she had trained at the same center in Colorado where Brianna trains."

"Cool!" The other girls were impressed.

"Really?" said Jamie. "That's a top training center."

"Coach Barnes even competed at nationals three times, but she never won or anything," said Kristen.

"How do you know all this stuff? She's not even your coach," said Shannon.

"Coach Grischenko told me."

Jamie was busy thinking. *Meeting Brianna Hill would be the highlight of my life.* "Do you think Coach Barnes might introduce us to her sometime?"

"I don't know," said Kristen.

"Isn't she going to be skating in that exhibition in Dallas next month?" asked Shannon.

Kristen nodded. "I think so. All the top skaters are coming."

"If Coach Barnes really knows her, you think she could introduce us then?" asked Amy.

"Yeah, that'd be *sooo* cool!" said Shannon.

Jamie didn't say anything. She knew if Brianna were to come to town, she was sure going to find some way to meet her.

Kristen pointed to a photograph. "Wow, here's a picture of her doing the triple axel."

"I'll be happy if I can just get a *single* axel!" moaned Shannon. Coach Barnes had recently begun teaching her the axel, the most difficult single jump. "So far all I do is fall! But I can do that better than anyone."

"Not me," said Kristen. "I'm pretty good at falling, too. Anyway, the axel is like that—nobody gets it right away."

"I did," said Jamie.

"How fast?" asked Shannon.

"About a week," said Jamie.

Kristen rolled her eyes. "Okay, I'll bite. How old?"

"Eight," said Jamie.

"No more!" said Amy emphatically. "It took me more than a year to land my first axel!"

"Come on, guys," teased Kristen. "Jamie probably doesn't want to hang around mere mortals like us." The girls turned and headed out of the store.

"Wait!" called Jamie. "I need to pay for my book."

Her friends came back while Jamie paid the cashier.

"Hey, can I read it after you?" asked Kristen.

"Sure," said Jamie.

"I've got dibs next," yelled Amy and Shannon at the same time. Then they all laughed.

Jamie tucked the book inside the sack. She couldn't wait to get home to read about her favorite skater.

❋ ❋ ❋ ❋ ❋

The boys were already there when Mrs. Grant and the girls arrived at the Tropical Cafe. There was a long line of people waiting to get a table, and Mrs. Grant told the kids to look around while she waited in line.

The restaurant was like a real rain forest, with the sounds of birds and animals and the rush of falling water.

"It looks like a jungle," said Jamie. "We don't have to eat some kind of health food, do we?"

"Well, they do have some 'jungle juices' and stuff like that," said Kristen. "But they have some junk food, too."

"Hey, look at this!" said Jamie, noticing a shelf of gag toys in the gift shop. "We could play some really good tricks on the boys!"

"Yeah," said Shannon.

"Don't let the guys know," said Kristen, lowering her voice. "Or they'll be playing tricks on *us!* We'll come back later."

"Table for Grant." The group followed the hostess into the restaurant to a table in a dark area underneath glowing stars. Mrs. Grant suddenly realized she was missing a shopping bag. "Oh, no! I put that bag down when I paid for a purchase at the department store. I'd better go back there right away. You kids can go ahead and order two large pizzas and some soft drinks. I'll be back as soon as I can."

Kevin poked Manuel. "It's so dark. We can't even see what we're eating!"

"Yeah," agreed Manuel. "You can't be too careful here."

"What do you mean?" demanded Kristen.

"You just want to make sure you don't accidentally eat something gross," said Kevin. "You know, this is like a real jungle, with insects and things."

"It's not!" protested the girls.

"I know a guy who ate a worm here," added Manuel.

"Didn't you notice all the birds and monkeys around the restaurant?" asked Kevin, winking at Manuel.

Jamie looked around. Sure enough, in the gift shop area there were a number of small live animals being displayed and cared for by employees. However, there were none in the restaurant itself.

"They wouldn't allow animals in a restaurant," countered Jamie.

"But this isn't an ordinary restaurant," said Kevin. He leaned forward, whispering, "You know, they keep all kinds of tropical animals in the gift shop. And some of them could get loose occasionally."

"I've never seen anyone buying any, but they do disappear," said Manuel.

Kevin lowered his voice dramatically. "You know, Jamie, if I were you, I'd be careful in here. You never know when you might see—A LIZARD!"

A green lizard slithered across the table. The girls screamed as they jumped from their seats, while Kevin and Manuel doubled over with laughter. "You fell for it!" Kevin bellowed.

The girls' faces turned bright red with embarrassment and anger. People in the restaurant were staring.

Kevin held up the rubber lizard.

"Just wait!" said Kristen. "When you least expect it!" She gave him a stern look.

"Excuse me, are you ready to order?" asked the waiter, who was dressed in safari-style shorts and shirt. "Our special today is monkey pizza . . ." The waiter looked baffled when the boys' mouths flew open. "It's not real monkey, guys. Just a name."

The group all started laughing.

Just as the pizza arrived, Mrs. Grant returned with her package. After lunch, she took the boys to get some jeans for Kevin. When they were out of sight, the girls made one final stop—at the gift shop's gag shelf.

❋ ❋ ❋ ❋ ❋

As soon as Jamie got home, she began reading her new book. The more she read, the more she realized how much Brianna's life had been like hers. Brianna had begun skating when she was three years old, and by the time she was twelve, she had won the novice championship in her region. At thirteen she had reached the junior level and could do all the triple jumps except the triple axel. Jamie wondered what it would be like to actually *be* a world champion like Brianna Hill.

This wasn't the first time Jamie had realized she had a lot in common with Brianna. And after all, Jamie had proved she could be a champion when she beat Tamara Vasiliev. Could she follow in Brianna's footsteps by becoming the national and world champion?

Jamie sighed and put away her book. It was almost time to go to bed, and she still had not read her Bible. She picked up her Bible, but her mind wasn't really on what she was reading. Instead, she kept seeing herself stepping on the podium to receive her gold medal. She wondered if God would help her reach her goal of becoming a world champion like Brianna Hill. She prayed, *Dear God, please help me to be the best skater in the world.*

Four

It was Monday morning at the skating rink, and Jamie had already had her lesson with Coach Grischenko. "You must practice these field moves," the coach had sternly instructed, shaking her head. "They are very important, Jamie. Jumps are good, but you must pass the moves test to go to the next level."

Jamie knew her coach was right. But moves in the field were so *boring.* It was much more fun to practice jumps.

After the coach left the rink for the morning, Jamie tried to obey her. Over and over she practiced the patterns, concentrating on speed and power. But all she could think of was how she needed to master those triple jumps. To be like Brianna Hill, she needed to master the triple flip and the triple lutz soon. Brianna had all her triple jumps by the time she was thirteen, and Jamie's thirteenth birthday was only a couple of months away.

In spite of what her coach said, Jamie was certain she could pass the field moves test easily. After all, she must be a pretty good skater to have defeated the national novice champion.

Besides, Jamie thought it was much more important to have great triple jumps to be competitive. Coach Grischenko had trained in the Ukraine years ago, when ballet moves were very important. She just didn't understand that nowadays you had to have lots of triple jumps to win championships.

I've done enough field moves for today, thought Jamie. She decided to work on the triple flip jump she had had trouble with in the competition. Gathering speed, she circled the rink, preparing to set up the jump. She skated forward and made a three turn onto the inside edge of her left foot, thrust her right toe pick into the ice behind her, and vaulted into the air. *Crash!* She hit the ice after only two and a half rotations.

Quickly, she hopped back on her feet and began the same procedure, setting up the jump. She was so intent on landing that jump that she didn't see Amy in her path until it was too late.

Crash! The two skaters collided and both went sprawling onto the ice. Jamie was the first to get up, and she immediately offered Amy her hand to help her. But Amy was in no mood to be forgiving.

"You should watch where you're going!" she cried, glaring at Jamie.

"Sorry!" said Jamie. "I didn't mean to run into you."

Amy got up slowly and limped to the side of the rink.

Jamie watched her go, hoping she wasn't hurt. At the same time, she thought Amy needed to stay out of her way. After all, Jamie was the one working on triple jumps.

A half-hour later Jamie got off the ice, pleased with the progress she was making on her triple flip. She found a bench in the lobby near her friends and began to take off her skates.

"Are you okay, Amy?" asked Jamie when she sat down.

Amy shrugged. "I guess so. But I'll be really sore tomorrow."

"I'm sorry," said Jamie. "It's kind of hard to work on triple jumps with so many skaters on the ice."

Amy gave her a funny look, but she didn't say anything.

"Jamie, we're all going to the exhibition next month," said Kristen. "Do you want to come, too?"

"That would be cool!" said Jamie. "Who's going to be skating—besides Brianna?"

"I hope Crystal Manning," said Shannon. "I love to watch her. She always does fun stuff."

"You mean like her Beach Boys routine?" Kevin showed up with his skate bag over his shoulder, ready to go. "I like it when she pretends to be the 'Little Old Lady from Pasadena.'" He hunched his shoulders in an imitation of Crystal performing as an old lady skating down the freeway, while he sang in a high voice: "'. . . and everybody's saying there's nobody meaner than the little old lady from Pasadena . . .'—hey, Kristen, you ought to skate to that music—you can look really mean when you want to!"

Kristen turned to him with a look of vengeance on her face.

"See! See! That's perfect!"

Kristen got up and started after Kevin, who beat a hasty retreat. Exasperated, she gave up on the chase and sat down to finish putting away her skates. "He's just showing off." She glanced at Shannon. "I think he likes you."

Shannon turned almost as red as the sweater she was wearing, but she didn't say anything. Jamie wondered if Shannon liked Kevin, too.

Amy laughed. "Well, he's got a funny way of showing it! He always does something dumb every time he's around us."

Kristen shook her head. "And you don't even see the stuff he does at home. Brothers!"

"Yeah," said Amy.

Jamie decided it was time to change the subject. "What day is the exhibition?" she asked Kristen.

"It's the last Friday in May," said Kristen.

"I can't wait to see Brianna!" said Jamie.

Kristen lowered her voice. "I heard she might be practicing here."

"You mean in Dallas?" asked Jamie.

"No, here," said Kristen. "I don't know for sure, but I overheard Coach Barnes say Brianna might practice some at the Ice Palace."

The girls looked at each other.

"That'd be awesome!" said Jamie.

"Maybe we could watch," suggested Amy.

"Coach Barnes might let us," said Shannon. "Maybe they *are* old friends."

"I'm going to ask," said Jamie.

Shannon looked puzzled. "But she's not even your coach."

"I know, but . . ." Jamie paused. She didn't want to sound conceited, but after all, she was the one most likely to be a champion skater like Brianna someday. "It's just that my skating is so much like Brianna's . . ." She trailed off, realizing her friends were staring at her.

Kristen looked at her watch. "Uh-oh, we're late." She picked up her bag. "Kevin, come on! See you guys later."

Everyone had gone except Jamie, but Mrs. Wells had not yet come for her. While Jamie waited, she thought of a plan. If Coach Barnes was still there, Jamie could talk to her about Brianna. Maybe Coach Barnes would arrange for Jamie to meet Brianna and watch her practice. Her friends had not understood why it was so important for her to meet the skating champion, but she was sure the coach would understand. After all, everybody knew that Jamie was preparing for a great skating career. Hadn't her mother moved here partly so that she could train with Coach Grischenko? And most important, hadn't she proved her ability to win important competitions?

Jamie saw a woman dressed in khaki pants and a light blue sweater emerge from the coaches' room. *It was Coach Barnes!* She looked different in regular clothes. Jamie was used to seeing her bundled up in a big coat and hat to keep warm while she gave lessons.

Jamie hesitated just an instant. After all, Coach Barnes *wasn't* her coach. But she was determined to at least find out whether it was really true that Brianna was coming to the Ice Palace to practice.

Jamie stood up as Coach Barnes entered the lobby. "Coach Barnes?" she said quietly.

"Yes, Jamie," the coach smiled. "Can I help you?"

Jamie cleared her throat and began. "Uh, is it true that you know Brianna Hill?"

"Yes."

"You really know her?"

"Yes, I do."

"Is she coming to Dallas to skate in the exhibition?"

The coach nodded. "Yes, that's true. I hope all of you will be able to go. There will be some really good skaters there, and Brianna will be one of them."

Jamie hesitated before she continued. Brianna's practice plans could have been just a rumor, after all. But Jamie had to find out. "We heard that Brianna might be practicing at the Ice Palace."

Coach Barnes frowned. "Where did you hear that?"

"Um, some of the kids said something about it." Jamie thought she had better not let the coach know it was Kristen. The coach didn't seem pleased.

Coach Barnes shifted the bag she was carrying. "Where the skaters have chosen to practice is not public information," she said. "They'll be performing for everyone at the exhibition. They don't need an audience when they practice."

"But since you are old friends," pleaded Jamie.

"For that reason alone, I must respect her privacy."

Coach Barnes was not being very cooperative, but Jamie wasn't ready to give up. "I just *have* to meet Brianna," she begged. "It's really important! She's the skater I most want to be like."

Coach Barnes looked at her thoughtfully for a moment. "If that's true, you've chosen a great role model. But if you want to be like Brianna, you must first learn to respect the rights of others." She thought for a moment. "I'm going to trust you with this information, but you are not to tell *anyone*. Is that clear?"

Jamie nodded, breathless.

The coach continued. "It is true that Brianna will be practicing at the Ice Palace. I was going to surprise my students with autographed pictures, and since you are so interested I will get one for you as well.

"But Brianna's practices will be during the day when you and your friends are at school. And they are *off-limits* to the public. Is that understood?"

"Yes, ma'am. Thank you." Jamie grabbed her skate bag and headed outside, where Mrs. Wells was waiting to take her to school.

Jamie was sure there was a way to meet Brianna. On the way to school she considered the problem. She was determined to meet Brianna and watch her skate. Even if she had to skip school to do it.

Five

"How's skating?" asked Heather when Jamie came into social studies class on Monday.

"Great!" answered Jamie as she sat down at her desk and pulled out her notebook. "I've even caught up on my homework for this class."

"I can't believe Mrs. Wise let you have extra time to get it in," whispered Heather.

"She's a really nice teacher," agreed Jamie. "Not like Miss Meyers."

Heather rolled her eyes. "I know what you mean. She's really strict. When I had a tooth removed, she called my mom and insisted she come pick up my homework so I could get it in the next week on time. I couldn't even eat, but I did my homework!"

Jamie nodded in agreement. "At my old school, we worked on our own, and there were teachers to tutor us. When I went to a competition, I just made up the work later."

"I wish I could go to a school like that," said Heather.

"I really miss it," sighed Jamie.

Jamie had always liked math and science best. She thought social studies was a boring subject, but Mrs. Wise made it interesting. She worked with Jamie on all her assignments, making sure Jamie could manage to complete them around her skating schedule.

Later that day in English class, Miss Meyers wasn't nearly as understanding. "Jamie, I would like to talk with you after class."

Jamie hoped Miss Meyers didn't want to talk about her book report. Jamie had handed in the report last Friday, as her teacher had required. However, the book Jamie had chosen to review had been very short.

"Jamie, you did not complete the assignment according to the guidelines I gave." Miss Meyers looked at her sternly. "The report was to have been on one of the books I listed. This book was not on the list because it is a book intended for younger students. It is not acceptable."

Jamie squirmed. "I'm sorry, Miss Meyers. I thought the list was just a list of suggestions."

Miss Meyers frowned. "I will not accept this report, because you did not follow instructions." She looked intently at Jamie. "I understand that you have a promising skating career?"

Jamie nodded uncertainly. This didn't sound like a compliment.

Miss Meyers went on. "I hope you understand that your education is more important than a possible skating career. You need to be as dedicated to your education as you are to your skating career. You might drop out of skating, but your education is forever."

Jamie listened in disbelief. *She sounds just like my mom. They just don't understand. Maybe that's true of most skaters, but I'm different. I really have a chance!*

Miss Meyers continued. "I am going to give you an opportunity to bring up your grade in this class. I would like for you to do a book report on one of the books on this list." She handed Jamie a paper that had a list of several books.

Jamie reluctantly took the list Miss Meyers handed her. She didn't need extra work just now.

"You *must* choose a book from this list. I'll expect your report in about two weeks. That will be Monday the . . ."

Great! More homework—I'll never catch up! Jamie thought as she wrote the date in her notebook.

Miss Meyers went on. "Now that this competition is out of the way, perhaps it is time to make your school-work a priority."

"Yes, ma'am." It didn't seem worthwhile to explain to her teacher that skating was far more important to her. Miss Meyers would never understand.

❋ ❋ ❋ ❋ ❋

Jamie had finished her skating practice early and was working on homework at the kitchen table when Mrs. Wells came into the room.

Mrs. Wells usually stayed until Jamie's mother came home in the evenings. Jamie liked the housekeeper.

With her white hair and pleasant face, she reminded Jamie of her own grandmother, whom she rarely saw.

"I don't like leaving you home alone," said Mrs. Wells, "but I promised my granddaughter I would be there for her birthday dinner tonight. Your mother said she'd be home no later than six, and it's almost six now."

Jamie looked up from doing her homework at the kitchen table. "It's okay if you want to leave now, Mrs. Wells. I'll be okay."

When Mrs. Summers had still not arrived at ten after six, Mrs. Wells called her office. After speaking to Jamie's mother for a few minutes, she reluctantly prepared to leave for her granddaughter's party. "Your mother promised to be home soon. She said you need to keep the doors locked until she gets here."

"I'll be fine," Jamie assured her.

Jamie took a break from her homework and logged on to the computer to check her e-mail. Laura, one of her friends from Atlanta, had sent her an e-mail telling about some of the things happening there. Reading it made her miss her old rink more than ever.

At 6:30 P.M. the phone rang. "Jamie, I just can't get away," her mother told her. "Has Mrs. Wells left?"

"Yes, but I'm fine," said Jamie. "I'm just working on the computer."

"It'll probably be another hour before I get there," said her mother. "I called Kristen's mother, and she said she would check on you in a little while."

"Okay, Mom." Discouraged, Jamie hung up the phone. Before her mother took this position, they spent a lot of time together. These days it seemed her mother had to stay later and later at the office.

She looked at the clock. It was almost 7:00 P.M. now. She had hoped her mother could take her to the library to get the book for her report. Jamie sighed. *I guess I won't get that book tonight.*

Besides, she was getting hungry. *I wonder what's for supper?* she thought to herself. *Maybe I could cook something and surprise Mom.*

She went to the refrigerator and looked to see what her mother had stocked. After some deliberation, she decided to make spaghetti. There was a packaged salad mix in the refrigerator and bottled spaghetti sauce. All Jamie had to do was cook the spaghetti and heat up the sauce.

Jamie put a large pot of water on the stove to boil. Then she set the table and put the salad in bowls. While she waited for the water to boil, she buttered a few slices of bread and sprinkled them with garlic powder. She put them on a tray and turned the oven to broil.

The water had started to boil, so Jamie dumped in the dried spaghetti to cook. She poured some of the spaghetti sauce in a saucepan and put it on the stove to heat.

After that things began to happen very quickly. Jamie wasn't sure how long the spaghetti needed to cook, but it looked as though it was done. She found the colander and poured the spaghetti and boiling water into it. Hearing a popping sound, she checked the spaghetti sauce only to find that she had had the heat on too high, causing the pan to scorch and the sauce to spatter all over the stove.

Sniff, sniff! Something was burning. *Oh, no! The garlic bread!* Jamie rushed to open the oven.

"Jamie, what's going on?"

Mrs. Summers came in to find the kitchen filled with smoke. She quickly opened a window and surveyed the disaster. Mrs. Summers took one look at the wrecked kitchen and at Jamie's woebegone face. Then she sat down and began to chuckle, shaking her head.

"Mom! Don't laugh!" complained Jamie, annoyed that her mother found the situation funny.

Her mother reached out and pulled Jamie to her and gave her a big hug.

"You wonderful child," she said.

Jamie pulled away and looked around at the disaster she had created, and she began to giggle along with her mom. Before she knew it, the two of them were sharing a good laugh, something they had not done since they had moved to Texas.

"Well, that's what I was planning to make. So, I guess it'll be Chinese takeout again tonight," said Mrs. Summers, grinning.

"Unless you want salad for supper," said Jamie, grinning. "I tried really hard, but I couldn't ruin that!"

Her mother gave Jamie a hug. "I'm sorry. I shouldn't have laughed. It was awfully sweet of you to try to make supper."

Jamie smiled. It almost seemed like old times to be

sharing a laugh with her mom, even if it was because of her disastrous cooking attempt.

It was late when Jamie and her mother finally sat down to their supper. "How was school today?" Mrs. Summers asked.

Jamie frowned. "Miss Meyers doesn't like me."

"What makes you say that?"

"She assigned me an extra book report."

Mrs. Summers glanced at her with lifted eyebrows. Jamie continued. "I'm having a hard time keeping up with my work. With my skating and competitions, I just can't get it all done."

"Then perhaps we had better cut down on your skating," said her mother.

"That's not fair!" protested Jamie. "You know how important my skating is to me."

"Jamie, I'm supportive of your skating, but school comes first."

The happy mood of the evening had disappeared. "I wouldn't have this problem in Atlanta," complained Jamie.

Her mother sighed. "Well, we're here now, and you might as well make the best of it," said Mrs. Summers. "Anyway, I expect to see an improvement in your schoolwork or I *will* inform Coach Grischenko that you're going to have to cut down on your practices."

Jamie put down her fork. "You don't even care. I needed to go to the library to get the book for that book report, but now it's too late!"

"I'm sorry, Jamie. But why didn't you ask Mrs. Wells to take you earlier?"

"I wanted you to take me."

Mrs. Summers sighed. "It couldn't be helped. You can get the book tomorrow night."

"But you're *never* here to help anymore. You used to help me with my homework, and we used to make dinner together. Now all we ever eat is takeout!"

Mrs. Summers ate silently. Finally, she spoke. "I'm sorry, Jamie. This is a new office, and I have more responsibilities here." She paused and looked hard at Jamie. "Things will get better, I promise."

Jamie took her dishes to the sink and started to leave the kitchen. "I wish we'd stayed in Atlanta!" she fumed, but her mother didn't seem to hear her.

Six

"Today, we will work on field moves," said Coach Grischenko, at the beginning of her lesson the next morning.

Oh, no, thought Jamie. *My favorite thing!*

Jamie skated each pattern required for the junior-level test. There were six patterns in all, and the coach insisted she skate them in order—just as if she were taking the test. Each pattern was somewhat different. Some required the skater to perform intricate turns with precision. Others required speed and power.

Jamie loved to jump and spin, but practicing footwork and patterns seemed dull to her. She knew she hadn't worked enough on these moves. The coach watched silently until she finished, then shook her head.

"No good." The coach's Ukrainian accent became thicker when she was displeased. "You are not ready."

"But I'm good enough to be a junior-level skater," protested Jamie. "I beat Tamara, didn't I?"

Coach Grischenko was not impressed. "The judges at the tests don't care if you win competitions. Field move patterns must be very good, or you will not pass."

"But I have to take this test soon!" Jamie was getting a little worried. She really wanted to move up to the junior level.

"Why?"

"I'll be thirteen soon."

"That is not important. We are not interested in your age," said Coach Grischenko. "No. Practice more."

For the rest of her lesson, the coach had Jamie work on field moves. "Bend your knees!" she shouted. "Extend your leg! More!"

Over and over, Jamie skated the patterns, until she was sick of them. She was relieved when the coach said, "Keep practicing, I have another student coming in."

That meant Coach Grischenko would be watching. Jamie continued to practice, but her heart wasn't in it. *Coach Grischenko is just picky*, she thought. *I'll bet I could pass this test tomorrow.* When the coach finally disappeared into the coaches' room, Jamie abandoned her field moves practice and launched into a rehearsal of her freestyle program.

Jamie had skated through her entire program, even landing a shaky triple flip jump, when she looked up to see Coach Grischenko on the ice staring at her with fire in her eyes.

Jamie knew her coach was unhappy with her for working on her program after she told her to practice field moves, but she didn't care. The coach crossed her arms and said, "This way, you will be thirty before you pass that test!"

Jamie decided that maybe it would be a good idea to go back to practicing her moves. Fortunately, the session was nearly over.

In order to compete as a junior, Jamie knew she needed to pass both the field moves test and a test on freestyle moves, such as jumps and spins. She wondered why her coach didn't want her to sign up for the skating test. Didn't she think Jamie was ready to compete at the junior level? But Jamie was absolutely certain she was ready to compete as a junior skater. After all, Brianna Hill was already competing as a junior by the time she was twelve years old. Maybe Coach Grischenko didn't think she was ready to compete at the junior level, but Jamie felt ready. *I wonder if I can sign up for the test even if my coach doesn't want me to?* Would she dare?

❋ ❋ ❋ ❋ ❋

Kristen already had her skates off when Jamie joined her in the lobby. "Hi, Jamie," said Kristen. "I saw you working on junior field moves in your lesson. Are you getting ready to take the junior test?"

Jamie nodded. "Yes. Coach Grischenko wants me to take it soon."

Kristen was impressed. "That's so cool! When?"

"Maybe next week." Jamie didn't think it was important to mention that Coach Grischenko hadn't yet given her approval.

"Jamie's going to move up to junior level!" Kristen told Amy and Shannon when they came in.

"Wow! I haven't even taken the test for the first of the seven levels tested," said Shannon.

"Well, after I pass the junior field moves, I'll still have to take the junior freestyle test," admitted Jamie. "But that should be pretty easy for me," she boasted. More and more Jamie felt certain that she should take the test soon. "Coach Grischenko thinks I have a great future. You know, I beat Tamara Vasiliev, and she's one of the best in the country."

Her friends exchanged glances.

"I can't wait to move up to the next level. Competing at novice level just isn't much of a challenge anymore. But you guys wouldn't know that," said Jamie.

"No, we wouldn't know," said Kevin, who had just gotten off the ice. "Since none of *us* have such a brilliant future," he added. Then putting out his forefinger he touched Jamie's shoulder and made a sizzling sound. "Yep, she's too hot for us." Then he left to join Manuel on the other side of the lobby.

Jamie ignored Kevin's sarcastic remark. He was probably just jealous. "I'm planning to take the test next week."

"Good luck," said Kristen. "I've heard the judges are really tough on those field moves tests. One mistake and that's it. Everything has to be perfect."

"My field moves will be perfect," said Jamie. "Coach Grischenko is going to see to that—even if I die of boredom!"

"I'm taking a test next month for intermediate. Maybe we could take our tests on the same day," said Amy.

"I can't believe it. You're moving up a level?" asked Jamie.

"The coach thinks I'm ready," said Amy, angry at Jamie's rude comment.

Jamie shook her head. "You're not ready."

Now, Amy was really offended. "Coach Grischenko says I am."

"Yeah, well . . . the competition is pretty tough," said Jamie. "And you can't do a double axel yet—"

"I guess I'll take the test when Coach Grischenko tells me to," said Amy, a little defensively.

The other girls silently continued preparing to leave. Jamie could tell they were annoyed with her, but she wasn't sure why. *I don't see why they're upset with me,* she thought. *All I did was tell Amy the truth. They're just jealous that I'm doing so well. Oh, well. That's the price of success.*

The other kids left, and Jamie finished putting away her skates. What if Coach Grischenko would not allow her to take the test? That would be embarrassing after boasting to her friends. Maybe she should sign up for the test herself. By the time the coach found out, Jamie would be ready and Coach Grischenko would be happy for her to take it.

Jamie went to the office and asked Mrs. Wysong, the rink secretary, for a test application. She filled out the application, but then she noticed it required Coach

Grischenko's signature. Jamie hesitated. Without the coach's signature, how could she sign up for the test?

Finally, Jamie decided she would submit the form anyway. Maybe no one would notice right away that Coach Grischenko's signature was missing. At least by the time the coach found out about it, Jamie would already be included on the test schedule. Then, surely the coach would agree.

Jamie gave the application to Mrs. Wysong and then she turned to go.

"Oh, wait, Jamie," said the secretary. "I need your coach's signature."

Jamie groaned inwardly. So much for her plan!

"That's okay," said Jamie. "She didn't have time to sign it this morning, but I can get her to sign it later."

"That's fine," said Mrs. Wysong. "But I'll need her signature before you take the test."

"Yes, ma'am," said Jamie. Now, if she could just convince Coach Grischenko to let her take the test!

✳ ✳ ✳ ✳ ✳

Where's Mom? thought Jamie. It was late afternoon, and Jamie had finished her after-school practice. Usually, Mrs. Wells picked her up in the afternoon, but today Mrs. Summers had promised to come. She and Jamie were planning to go to the library for the book Jamie needed. Then they would go out to eat. Jamie had been waiting for half an hour already, and there was no sign of her mother.

Finally, she saw Mrs. Wells's car coming into the parking lot of the rink. Jamie's heart sank. *Why hadn't her mother come?*

"Your mother called and asked me to pick you up from the rink," Mrs. Wells explained when Jamie got into the car. "Something came up, and she couldn't get away."

"But she promised she'd come home early tonight!" said Jamie, disappointment written all over her face.

"I'm sorry, dear," said Mrs. Wells sympathetically. "Your mom has a very important job."

"Yeah," mumbled Jamie. "More important than me."

✽ ✽ ✽ ✽ ✽

Jamie got right to work on her homework as soon as she got home. She was still trying to catch up on all the work she had missed when she was preparing for the last competition.

The phone rang, and Jamie heard Mrs. Wells answer it.

"Jamie, that was your mother," called Mrs. Wells a few minutes later. "She's having to work very late tonight, and she asked me to make you some supper. I'll stay until she gets home."

"Thanks, Mrs. Wells," answered Jamie. The house-keeper fixed some macaroni and cheese and a salad for her. Jamie ate her supper and went back to her home-work. She sighed as she tackled the homework for math class. She missed having her mother around these days. Ever since she was little, they had done everything together. Jamie couldn't remember ever having her father around. She was very small when he left. She had seen him occasionally through the years. He always remembered holidays. And they exchanged letters and phone calls. Still, she did not know him very well. Sometimes she longed for him and wondered what he was doing.

Mrs. Summers had supported Jamie in everything, including her skating career. She had made sure Jamie had lessons with excellent coaches, plenty of time to practice at the rink, and proper skates and costumes. She had spent hours driving Jamie to and from the rink or hired housekeepers or sitters to drive her. Now, however, her mother didn't even seem interested in Jamie's skating. She had even threatened to cut down on Jamie's skating if she didn't keep her grades up at school. But she wasn't here to help her with her homework! Jamie began to realize that if she wanted to succeed in skating, she was on her own.

She looked at the clock. It was almost 9:00 P.M.— too late to go to the library. Jamie finished all her other homework, put her books away, and began to get ready for bed.

After climbing into bed, Jamie took her Bible from the night table. Although she had promised to read a little in it every night, she hadn't done very well about keeping that promise. In fact, she had hardly touched it since she got home from the competition. She was already very tired, but she flipped through the pages looking for a short chapter or verse to read before she went to sleep.

The first verse in Hebrews 12 caught her eye: "So we have many people of faith around us. Their lives tell us what faith means. So let us run the race that is before us and never give up. We should remove from our lives anything that would get in the way."

Jamie stopped reading there. This verse sounded like it was meant just for her. God could help her with her skating!

Jamie had an important goal in her life, and that goal was to win national and world championships, and one day the Olympics. The way to reach that goal was to put everything else aside. Nothing else mattered.

Dear God, I want to be a champion more than anything else in the world! Please help me to focus on my goal. If You will help me, I know I can do it! Amen.

Seven

Jamie could tell Coach Grischenko was angry. Her piercing blue eyes bored into her as soon as she stepped onto the ice the next morning.

"You signed up for the test without my permission. Why?" she demanded.

Jamie's confidence wavered just a little. The coach was *really* mad! "I thought you wanted me to take the test soon. If I work really hard on my field moves, I know I can be ready."

"I am the coach. *I* make the decisions!" the coach went on. "Do you understand?"

"Yes, ma'am." Jamie gulped. She hadn't imagined Coach Grischenko would get so angry about a test session.

"I think you are not ready for this test. You think you are. Very well," said the coach. "If you insist on taking the test, you will test now. We will see who is right. Pass or fail, it is up to you!"

By the time her lesson was over, Jamie wished she had never heard of moves in the field—or Coach Grischenko! The coach worked every move over and over, criticizing every tiny detail of Jamie's skating.

At the end of the morning practice, Jamie practically crawled into the lobby and landed in a heap on the benches near her friends.

"What's wrong?" asked Shannon, concerned.

Jamie groaned. "I never thought it was possible to work so hard on ordinary field moves," she complained.

"What's up with the coach?" asked Kristen. "My lesson was right after yours, and she was on a warpath! I couldn't do anything to please her!"

Jamie shrugged. "I don't know." She couldn't tell her friends that she had signed up for the test without the coach's permission.

"I hope she's in a better mood for my lesson tomorrow," said Amy as she put her skates away. "Hey, did you guys see the poster on the bulletin board?" she asked, pointing to a huge picture of a skater.

"What poster?" asked Kristen, scanning the bulletin board. "Oh, look, it's a picture of Brianna Hill." She zipped her skate bag closed and walked over for a closer look. "It's about the exhibition tour."

"Cool!" said Jamie as she limped over to look with one skate still on. "I can't wait to see her."

"Yeah, and all the other skaters," said Shannon. "Mom even promised Tiffany she could go. It's going to be so great!"

"I wonder if we can get Brianna's autograph?" asked Amy. "After all, Coach Barnes knows her."

Jamie sat down near the poster to take off her other skate. "*I* intend to do more than get her autograph," she said. "I'm going to meet her."

The other girls stared at her. "How are you going to do that?" Amy asked curiously.

"Oh, I'm just talking," said Jamie, afraid she'd let her secret almost slip out. "I'm still hoping Coach Barnes might let me come watch her practice."

"She's not even your coach," said Shannon. "Why would she let *you* in to watch Brianna, and not her own students?"

"Well, I'm already competing in important championships, you know," said Jamie. "I need to talk to advanced skaters like Brianna so I can get advice on how to handle all that pressure."

Jamie ignored the surprised looks on her friends' faces. If they were jealous because she was such a good skater, that was *their* problem.

"Well, she'll never let you watch the practice," said Kristen. "It's supposed to be private. Besides, she's practicing while we're all in school."

Jamie was a little disappointed that Kristen had so much information. She thought she was the only one who knew about that. "I get out of school a lot earlier than you guys. But I would skip school for a chance to meet Brianna."

"Yeah, me, too. But my parents would be really

mad and I'd be grounded for life," said Amy. "Maybe we can wait around before the ice show. Sometimes the skaters give autographs."

"Yeah, maybe," said Jamie. But inside she knew she wouldn't be satisfied just to get an autograph.

❄ ❄ ❄ ❄ ❄

"Did you finish your report on the Alamo?" asked Heather when Jamie came into social studies class later that morning.

Jamie dropped her books on her desk. "Oh, no!" she cried. "I forgot that was due today." She sat down and put her face in her hands.

Heather shook her head. "Jamie, you're going to be in big trouble! Not even Mrs. Wise will give that much special treatment."

"I know," sighed Jamie. "I've had a lot of other homework. And I've been so busy with skating . . ."

"That's all you ever think about, isn't it?" Heather asked.

Jamie sighed. "Yeah, I'm kind of addicted. It takes a lot of time."

Heather looked hard at Jamie. "You know, you're not the only one in this whole school who has a life. We're all busy, but we don't all expect special treatment."

"Oh, I'm sorry, Heather," Jamie said, but she really didn't mean it. *After all, what does Heather have to do?* Jamie thought. *I wonder why everyone is always so mad at me. I guess they are just jealous.*

Mrs. Wise was one of the nicest teachers in school, but she expected assignments to be turned in on time. When Jamie asked for more time to do the report, she frowned. "Jamie, it's not fair for you to have more time than the other students. I know your training takes a lot of time, but other students have outside activities, too." She sighed. "This time I am taking fifteen points off your grade. And this is the last time I'm accepting a late assignment from you. Is that clear?"

"Yes, ma'am."

"Tough luck," whispered Heather rather sympathetically despite her earlier comments. "She did the same thing to me when I competed in a horse show."

Jamie smiled back weakly. So, Heather rides horses sometimes. She just wouldn't understand how hard it is to travel all the time. Things just weren't going well at all today. First, Coach Grischenko was angry with her. Now, it was Mrs. Wise, the only teacher who had been understanding about her skating. What next?

❋ ❋ ❋ ❋ ❋

Mrs. Summers came home early that evening with a homestyle-cooked meal from a local restaurant. "Mmm," said Jamie when she smelled the food. She opened the boxes to find roast beef and gravy, mashed potatoes, peas, rolls, and a green salad. "This looks good! What's the occasion?"

Her mother smiled. "No special reason. I just thought we needed a good meal tonight."

"I'll set the table," Jamie volunteered. Maybe her mother hadn't cooked, but after her terrible day, the familiar food made her feel better.

A few minutes later Jamie and her mother sat down to share their meal. "By the way," said Mrs. Summers, "I've been trying to get in touch with that piano teacher. I hope to set up some lessons soon."

"Oh, no hurry," said Jamie.

"How was skating today?"

"Okay, I guess," said Jamie. "I'm supposed to take the test for junior field moves a week from Saturday."

"Hmm, when is that?" Her mother glanced at the calendar hanging in the kitchen. "On the fourteenth?"

Jamie nodded.

"Oh, honey, I won't be able to be there. I'm sorry."

Jamie's smile faded. Her mother had always been there for her skating tests. "Why not?" she asked.

"There's a seminar that day for my department," she explained. "Since I'm in charge, I have to be there."

"Couldn't you try?" pleaded Jamie. "I'll ask if they can schedule my test early."

Her mother shook her head. "No, I'll need to be in the office early to be sure everything is set up. I doubt you'll be finished in time for me to do both."

"It's all because of this new job!" Jamie complained. "You never have time for me anymore!"

"I'm sorry, Jamie," her mother said. "I've got an idea. Could you wait until the next test session?"

Jamie shook her head. "No, I can't take the freestyle test for junior level until I pass the field moves part."

"Then you'll have to do this one without me. I'll try to be there for your junior freestyle test. Okay?"

"I guess so." Jamie ate in silence. This day had already been so bad that it didn't seem as though anything else could go wrong.

But things got worse.

The phone rang, and Mrs. Summers answered it.

"Hello. . . . Oh, yes, Mrs. Gomez."

Jamie froze. She didn't mean to eavesdrop, but she couldn't help overhearing. Mrs. Gomez was the principal of Westbridge Academy. There was a long silence while her mother listened. Finally, Mrs. Summers spoke.

"I completely agree. I'll make sure Jamie understands the consequences if her work doesn't improve."

Oh, no, I'm sunk! thought Jamie.

Mrs. Summers hung up the phone with a sharp click. She turned to Jamie.

"That was your principal. She tells me that you are having a difficult time keeping up with your classes."

"It was just the competition, Mom. I got behind, and I can't seem to catch up."

Mrs. Summers sat down at the table and looked at Jamie. "Jamie, I want you to understand that this will *not* continue. As much as I support your skating training, I cannot allow you to fall behind in your schoolwork."

"This school just isn't right for me," said Jamie. "The teachers won't help me the way the teachers at my old school did."

Her mother sighed. "Your old school was especially for kids in stage and professional athletic training.

67

There just isn't a school like that available right now. Westbridge has allowed you time to practice and travel to competitions. I'm sure you can keep up with the work."

"I don't see why I should even have to go to school," grumbled Jamie. "Lots of the top competitors have tutors."

"I considered that option," her mother reminded her. "With my work schedule, it simply isn't the best choice for you right now. You would have to spend your entire day with tutors and Mrs. Wells. You wouldn't be able to take part in any homeschool activities."

"I didn't know how hard Westbridge was going to be," said Jamie. "Can't we get tutors for me now?"

"No," said her mother firmly. "You're going to stay at Westbridge—at least until the end of the school year. After that, we'll see. But in the meantime, your school-work comes first. If things don't improve, you will lose computer and television privileges for two weeks, and you will have to drop your afternoon skating practices."

Jamie stared at her mother, horrified. She couldn't possibly mean what she had just said. To cut down on her skating practice, even for a few weeks, was the ultimate punishment for a future star like Jamie.

Eight

It was still dark when Jamie walked into the rink early on Thursday morning, but the air outside was pleasantly cool and smelled of spring. With all the other problems she was having right now, she looked forward to seeing her friends these days. *At least my friends will understand,* she thought.

However, Jamie didn't see any of the girls when she arrived. Kevin was playing video games, his skates already on, so Kristen had to be around somewhere.

"Hi, Jamie!" called Kevin in his friendly way. Jamie smiled back as she began her stretching and warmup routine. It was quiet in the lobby of the rink. There were several kids already skating and two or three small girls in the lobby lacing their skates. Manuel was on the ice, but Jamie didn't see Kristen or Amy. Shannon didn't skate early on Thursdays.

The door to the girls' bathroom opened and Jamie heard Kristen's and Amy's voices coming from inside.

"Do you think Shannon can go to the planetarium with us?" she heard Kristen ask.

"I'll ask her this morning at school," said Amy.

"I hope she can go," said Kristen. "That new show about the planets sounds pretty cool. Maybe we should invite Jamie. She really likes stuff like that."

"Why should we invite her?" asked Amy scornfully. "She's so stuck-up lately!"

"Yeah," admitted Kristen. "But if I were as good a skater as she is, I might be a little conceited, too."

"You're too kind, Kristen. Did you hear what she said to Shannon the other day?" asked Amy. "Shannon wore a new skating dress—and Jamie practically told her it was ugly!"

"You know Jamie always says what she thinks."

Just at that moment the girls came out of the bathroom and saw Jamie sitting in the lobby. They looked at each other uncomfortably, but didn't say anything.

"Hi, Jamie," said Kristen softly as she and Amy sat down and began to lace up their skates.

Jamie just nodded. She finished putting on her skates and headed for the ice. What Amy said really hurt. Did her friends truly think she was stuck-up?

Jamie couldn't see why they thought she was conceited. She was proud of her skating, and she didn't think she had said anything that wasn't true. Still, it hurt that they were excluding her from their trip to the planetarium. Especially since Jamie loved astronomy. She would have done anything to be included. Except ask—not after what Amy said!

Amy and Kristen hardly said a word while they put on their skates, but Jamie could tell by their faces that they were afraid she had overheard them.

Jamie didn't have a lesson scheduled for that morning, but Coach Grischenko had told her to work only on field moves. Her test was a week from Saturday. Jamie dreaded the thought of a whole morning session spent only on field moves, but she decided to practice them before she did any jumps or spins.

For forty-five minutes Jamie did the junior field move patterns over and over. The first two patterns were not too difficult for her. *Bent knees,* Jamie reminded herself while she skated the circular patterns. She was fairly pleased when she finished the first two patterns, so she went on to the next two.

These were more difficult. Both patterns required an intricate turn called a rocker. Jamie had had trouble with these. She could do these turns easily by themselves, but when she skated the pattern she couldn't seem to complete them with the precision and quickness the coach wanted from her.

Before she came to work with Coach Grischenko, Jamie thought she was performing the field move patterns correctly. Now that the coach had shown her the right way to do the turns, Jamie realized that she had learned them wrong. Now she couldn't seem to get them right. Jamie couldn't remember ever being so frustrated over her skating.

I'm going to get this! Jamie decided. She went through both patterns once more, but although she tried her best, she wasn't sure they would pass the test. Finally, she stopped, angry with herself for failing.

Jamie didn't feel like skating anymore that morning. *I'm never going to get this!* she thought. Then a new realization hit her. *What if I don't pass this test? I won't be able to move up to junior level!*

Jamie took off her skates and waited for Mrs. Wells. There was only a week left before the test session. Maybe Coach Grischenko was right—maybe she wasn't ready for the test yet. It would be so humiliating to fail, especially after she had bragged to her friends about passing the junior level tests.

Jamie had never failed a skating test before—something few skaters could say. And she didn't want that record shattered now.

❋ ❋ ❋ ❋ ❋

The day had gotten off to a bad start, and things continued to go wrong at school. Jamie walked into English class apprehensively. She had finally gotten the book for her book report, but she hadn't managed to write the composition assigned for today. She wondered why it was always so hard to finish her English homework. She never seemed to have trouble getting her math and science homework done.

When Miss Meyers asked for homework papers, Jamie cringed. Since she had to do the extra book report in addition to her regular work, she had hoped she could have extra time to finish the composition.

"I'm sorry, Miss Meyers," she admitted. "I will have it finished by tomorrow, I promise!"

"No, it will be done today," said the teacher firmly. "I will arrange a study hall for you after your last class, and you will stay there until you finish the work."

"But I have skating practice!" protested Jamie.

"You'll have to skip it today," said the teacher crisply. "I'll contact your mother to let her know you're staying late at school. Jamie, you have had many warnings. It is time to take your schoolwork seriously. Even a famous ice skater needs an education!"

Jamie groaned. Her mother would be furious! And Coach Grischenko would never understand.

She heard a low titter run through the class and Jamie realized some of the kids were laughing at her. She slumped in her desk, annoyed at having to put up with such juvenile behavior. When she became a world champion skater—she'd show them all!

❄ ❄ ❄ ❄ ❄

Usually, Jamie left school right after lunch, which was far earlier than the other students. However, today Jamie spent the afternoon in the school library working on her unfinished assignment for Miss Meyers's class. Jamie couldn't see why the teacher had to be such a bear!

Jamie finally finished her paper and handed it in. She headed to her locker, but when she got there she found a banner draped across the front. "World

Champion Dummy," it read. A crudely drawn ice skater with a silly expression completed the humiliating picture. Jamie reached up and tore the banner off her locker. Just as she did so, she heard a group of boys break into laughter and hurry off.

Jamie stood there with the torn banner in her hands, feeling humiliated. So *this* was what the other kids at this school thought of her!

❈ ❈ ❈ ❈ ❈

For once Jamie was glad her mother had to work late. Since she had had to skip afternoon skating practice, Jamie spent the rest of the afternoon working on other homework. It was surprising how much she could accomplish when she worked hard. She had nearly caught up in all her subjects!

She could tell her mother was angry as soon as she walked in the door that evening. "Jamie, we need to have a serious talk."

Jamie reluctantly put down her science textbook and faced her mother.

Mrs. Summers sighed deeply. "I was very disappointed when I received the call from your school this afternoon, especially since we had discussed this issue several times." She stared at Jamie a few moments before continuing. "Jamie, I know how important your skating is to you. However, I warned you that if you continued to have trouble keeping up with your schoolwork, you would have to cut down on your skating practices."

"But I'm almost caught up now!" said Jamie in a panic. "I've worked hard all afternoon! I can't cut down now—I've got the skating test next week!"

Her mother shook her head. "I don't know what to do! You've always been a good student before!"

"The problem is my school," said Jamie. "Westbridge just isn't right for me. I think it's time to quit school and get a tutor! Like Brianna Hill."

"Jamie, we've discussed this. The answer is no. With my long hours at work, you would be too isolated."

"Your job! That's the only thing that matters to you!" retorted Jamie. "You don't care about me anymore!"

"That's not true and you know it!" said her mother sharply. "Jamie, for the next week you are to drop your afternoon skating practices."

"How am I going to pass the test if I can't practice?"

"Right now it's more important that you pass the seventh grade!" said her mother. "You can still practice in the morning sessions."

It just isn't fair! Jamie thought to herself. *Nobody understands—not even Mom!*

Nine

Coach Grischenko wasn't at all happy that Jamie couldn't come to her afternoon skating practice. When she found out the reason, she gave Jamie a stiff lecture. "If you wish to be a great skater," said the coach, "you must learn discipline in all areas of your life, not just skating."

Jamie listened unhappily. She thought Coach Grischenko would be on *her* side.

The coach folded her arms and looked sternly at Jamie. "You will work hard—very hard—every morning."

Coach Grischenko was as good as her word. Jamie had no choice but to work on her field moves every morning. The coach watched every move Jamie made. Even while the coach was giving a lesson to other students, Jamie knew she was also watching her.

Even so, when Jamie skated the field move patterns on Friday morning Coach Grischenko shook her head and sighed. "Maybe you will pass, maybe not."

"I've never failed a skating test," said Jamie.

"Perhaps the judges will be kind. Be here at eight o'clock tomorrow morning," the coach said.

❋ ❋ ❋ ❋ ❋

The rest of the day seemed to go on forever. Jamie found it difficult to concentrate. All she could think about was the test tomorrow.

"Jamie, may I see you for a moment?" asked Miss Meyers at the end of English class.

Jamie gulped. "Yes, ma'am." Again, she had forgotten all about the book report!

When the bell rang, Jamie gathered her books and reported to the teacher's desk. She dreaded the conference because she knew what it was about.

"I assigned this report, hoping it would help to bring up your grades," said the teacher. "I'm expecting to see a quality report handed in on time."

"Yes, ma'am," answered Jamie. But her thoughts were spinning. *How am I ever going to finish that report with the test tomorrow?*

Heather waited for Jamie in the hallway. "What did Miss Meyers want to see you about?" she asked anxiously.

Jamie was touched by her friend's concern. "She assigned me a special book report."

"What's the problem?" asked Heather.

"It's due Monday, and I haven't even finished reading it. I've been so busy with skating."

"Oh!" Heather gave her a look of sympathy. "Is there anything I can do to help?"

"Thanks," sighed Jamie. "But I guess I'll just have to get it done somehow."

✽ ✽ ✽ ✽ ✽

That night Jamie tried to read, but her mind kept returning to the skating test. *What if I don't pass?*

Jamie took her new Bible off the night table and flipped through the pages, but the words didn't sink in. It was no use. She had only one thing on her mind. Jamie rested her chin on her hand and prayed: *Dear Lord, please help me pass this test. Amen.*

✽ ✽ ✽ ✽ ✽

It was quiet at the rink on the morning of the test. Jamie warmed up with some stretching exercises and running in place before she put on her skates. Coach Grischenko and the other coaches were having coffee and talking. A few other skaters were lacing up their skates.

Jamie felt all alone. Her mother had gone to the office very early that morning, and none of Jamie's friends had come to the rink to support her. She remembered that this was the day they were going to the planetarium—without her.

Jamie looked at the row of skating judges seated by the side of the rink. At her old rink, she had known all the skating officials and judges. In Walton the judges and test officials were all strangers.

Most skating judges are nice people who try hard to judge fairly. Still, it is difficult to do your best when you know there is a row of people at the side of the rink watching every move you make. Jamie felt a cold chill run through her, and it wasn't from the air in the arena.

"Remember to extend your leg and point your toe," Jamie's coach reminded her while they waited.

Jamie listened anxiously. For the first time since she had been skating she wasn't sure she could pass.

Finally, it was Jamie's turn to skate. Nervously, she took her place on the ice, waiting for the signal to begin. There were three judges: one man with a beard, a young woman with French-braided hair, and a gray-haired older woman. The three stared at her unsmilingly, waiting with pencils in hand to note every slight mistake in technique. Jamie glanced toward Coach Grischenko for encouragement, then began skating the first pattern.

Although she was nervous, Jamie tried to appear calm and confident. She had never failed a test before, and she didn't intend to fail this one. She smiled at the judges and skated as though she were performing for an audience.

After each of the six patterns, Jamie paused, waiting for the test chairman to signal for her to begin the next pattern. When she finally finished the test, she felt an enormous sense of relief. She was glad it was over.

Coach Grischenko made no sign when Jamie got off the ice. *This is not good,* thought Jamie. She could tell Coach Grischenko wasn't happy with the way she had skated, but she hoped the judges disagreed.

Jamie went back to the lobby and began unlacing her skates. A few minutes later she saw Coach Grischenko coming into the lobby with a sheet of paper.

"You did not pass," said the coach.

Jamie felt as if her world had ended. She had *failed!* She couldn't believe it.

Coach Grischenko was not very sympathetic. "You were not ready, as I told you. Perhaps now you will work harder."

Jamie felt dismal. There was no one to comfort her. *How will I ever get to be a champion?* she wondered.

Jamie hardly said a word while Mrs. Wells drove her home from the rink. She couldn't believe she had failed. Since she started skating, she had amazed everyone with her abilities. Everyone but Coach Grischenko.

Maybe her coach was the problem. Jamie was sure she should have been able to pass that test by now. Maybe she would have been ready for the test if she had still been taking lessons with Emily at her old rink.

❋ ❋ ❋ ❋ ❋

Jamie spent the afternoon alone in her room. She knew she should be reading the book for her report, but she just didn't feel like it. She glanced at her new Bible on the night table, but she left it where it was. She had asked God to help her pass the test, and He hadn't answered. *How could God have deserted her just when she needed Him most?*

Ten

Jamie found it hard to join in the Sunday morning service. All during the sermon her mind was on one thing: reaching her goal of being a national and world champion figure skater. But first she had to catch up on her schoolwork.

Then Pastor Carter's sermon caught her attention: "Just follow Jesus. That's the way to win. If anything gets in the way of following Jesus, get rid of it! *Nothing* is more important than living for the Lord!"

Jamie thought about that for a minute. *That's okay for Pastor Carter. That's all he has to do,* she thought. *Skating was different.* She smiled to herself. *And Coach Grischenko would never understand about putting Jesus before skating either!*

❄ ❄ ❄ ❄ ❄

Jamie read all afternoon and finally finished her report at nine that night. She sighed with relief when she put it into her notebook to hand in the next day at school. At least for now she had caught up on her schoolwork. She was annoyed she had to spend all day Sunday working on homework.

Jamie hurriedly undressed and climbed into bed. Five A.M. came early and she needed to get to sleep. But sleep didn't come right away. For a long time she lay awake thinking about skating and school and her friends. She realized she was paying a heavy price to reach her goal of becoming a champion skater. Was it really worth it?

❄ ❄ ❄ ❄ ❄

Shannon, Amy, and Kristen were already at the rink when Jamie arrived early the next morning. They greeted her briefly when she came in, but didn't pay her any further attention.

"Coach Barnes said it's true: Brianna will be practicing here at the Palace," Shannon was telling them. "But it will be while we're at school, and nobody's allowed at her practice anyway."

Amy looked disappointed. "Maybe if we talked to Coach Barnes, we could convince her to let us watch."

"Yeah, we could promise not to make any noise," said Kristen.

Shannon looked doubtful. "No. Coach Barnes told all her students that Brianna's practices are off-limits."

"I guess we can only see her at the exhibition," said Kristen.

"Coach Barnes did promise to get everyone an autographed picture," said Shannon.

"Cool!" said Amy.

"What's the big deal about an autographed picture?" asked Jamie.

The other girls stared at Jamie in disbelief.

Jamie shrugged. "A picture's okay, but I've got to meet Brianna herself."

"Good luck," said Kristen as she headed through the doors to the rink.

Amy and Shannon finished lacing up their skates without saying anything. Jamie could tell they were annoyed with her, but she didn't really understand why.

Jamie finished lacing her skates and headed to the ice for her lesson with Coach Grischenko. She expected a scolding for the failed test, but the coach greeted her without commenting on it. "Let's work on those junior moves again," she said simply.

For the next half-hour, Jamie and her coach went over every move in the test. At the end of the lesson Coach Grischenko gave her an approving nod. "Much better. I think you take the test seriously now." She paused for a moment, thinking. Then she said, "Next month, you will take the test again. It is like life, Jamie. You must work hard to pass. I think if you work hard you will be ready next month. You may sign up—with my permission this time."

Jamie smiled and nodded. She understood what the coach meant. She had finally realized how important it was to work hard on practicing these field moves. Now she knew she would be able to pass this test the next time. She was pleased that the coach thought so, too.

After practice that morning Jamie went to Mrs. Wysong's office to sign up for the next test session. When Jamie came in, the secretary was on her way out of the office carrying a stack of papers. "I'll be right back, Jamie," she said. "Just wait right there."

Jamie sat down on a chair to wait, but Mrs. Wysong didn't come back right away. After a few minutes, Jamie grew restless. She looked around the office curiously, trying to pass the time. She didn't mean to snoop, but when she spotted a note on the desk with *Brianna Hill* written in red ink she couldn't help but look. "Schedule change for Thursday, May 26. Afternoon freestyles canceled."

Jamie knew that Brianna Hill would be in town next week for the exhibition. *That must be when Brianna is practicing!* thought Jamie. There couldn't be any other reason for the freestyles to be canceled, and Coach Barnes had said Brianna would be practicing during school hours.

Most of the kids will be in school, but not me, Jamie thought. *I always come early and I could come even earlier that day. Mrs. Wells wouldn't know the freestyles had been canceled.* Jamie could barely conceal her excitement. *I'm going to meet Brianna!*

❊ ❊ ❊ ❊ ❊

"Here's my book report, Miss Meyers," Jamie said as she handed in her assignment that morning.

The teacher took the report and glanced at it, then smiled at Jamie. "Very good," she said. "This should help to bring up your grade in this class."

"Yes, ma'am," said Jamie. She had never realized what a pretty smile Miss Meyers had. She turned to go back to her desk.

"Wait, Jamie!" said Miss Meyers. "I would like to talk to you about another assignment."

What now? thought Jamie, frowning.

"The school year is almost over, but I am going to assign the class a research project."

Not another research paper! thought Jamie.

Miss Meyers continued. "The other students will do a report on a famous author, but I would like you to do something a little different. Would you be interested in writing a report on the history of skating?"

Jamie's face lit up. This sounded more interesting. "Yes, ma'am," she answered.

"Good! Would you like to present your report to the class? You could bring some of your skating memorabilia to make a display. You will receive extra credit."

Jamie nodded. At last, an English assignment she could get interested in!

Eleven

"Remember," said Coach Grischenko at the end of Jamie's lesson on Thursday the following week, "the afternoon freestyle times are canceled today."

Jamie nodded, smiling to herself. Notices had been posted the day before, but no one had said anything about the reason for the cancellation. Only Jamie was certain she knew the truth: Brianna's practice session.

While she took off her skates she reviewed her strategy. Jamie had not mentioned the change in the schedule to either her mother or Mrs. Wells. When Mrs. Wells dropped her off at the rink as usual that afternoon, Jamie would sneak into the rink and hide under the bleachers. She would try to talk to Brianna after she finished her practice.

Amy and Shannon came into the lobby, chattering about the exhibition.

"I can't wait to see Brianna skate tomorrow night!" said Shannon, sitting down on the bench near Jamie.

"Are you going to the exhibition, Jamie?"

Jamie nodded. "There's no way I would miss that!"

"We're going early to try and get some autographs from some of the skaters," said Kristen, joining them.

"Maybe we'll even see them warming up on the ice," said Amy.

"Yeah, that's going to be so cool!" said Shannon. She turned to Jamie. A little uncertainly, she asked, "Maybe you'd like to come?"

"Maybe," replied Jamie. "But I'm not interested in just autographs. I want to meet Brianna in person."

The other girls looked at her in surprise. "You'd have to meet her in person to get her autograph," said Kristen.

"How else can you meet her?" asked Amy.

Jamie shrugged and continued putting away her skates. "I've already made arrangements." She stood up to leave.

"What about us? Can we meet her, too?" asked Shannon.

Jamie shook her head. "No. This is a private meeting." Then, trying to get back at her friends for how rude they had been to her, Jamie boasted, "It's already been arranged."

"Wow," said Shannon, disappointed.

Kristen zipped her skate bag closed. "Come on, Kevin!" she called to her brother. She turned to go, followed by Amy and Shannon.

Jamie watched them leave, feeling left out. *They didn't say good-bye!* she realized. *Never mind!* she told herself. *When I'm a famous skater, they won't ignore me.*

The parking lot at the rink was nearly empty when Mrs. Wells arrived with Jamie later that day. "It looks like no one's here," commented the housekeeper. "Do you see your coach's car?"

Coach Grischenko drove a small red sports car, but there was no sign of it. Of course, Jamie hadn't expected her to be there. "No," said Jamie. "But she said she might be late."

Mrs. Wells seemed a little hesitant about leaving Jamie at the nearly deserted rink. "Are you sure you have practice this afternoon?" she asked. "I'm not sure I should leave you here."

"It's okay," said Jamie. "Mrs. Wysong's here. That's her white car over there."

Mrs. Wells pulled up to the door and Jamie got out. "All right, but call me if your coach doesn't show up. I'll be at your house for about thirty minutes, then I need to do some shopping. Have a good practice."

"Thanks, Mrs. Wells." Jamie hoped no one saw them drive up, but if anyone questioned her about being there she could just tell them she forgot that the practices were canceled. She opened the door and went into the lobby, but no one seemed to be around. The ice surface was empty; there was no sign of Brianna Hill.

Jamie slipped into the arena, feeling conspicuous lugging her big skate bag. She found a spot behind the metal bleachers and waited, hoping it wouldn't be long before Brianna arrived. It was cold under the bleachers and there was no place to sit. There was nothing to do, so she just waited, shivering alone in the cold air of the rink. She wondered if she had it all wrong. Perhaps Brianna wasn't practicing this afternoon after all.

After what seemed like forever, Jamie heard voices. Coach Barnes and Brianna were coming into the rink, laughing and talking like old friends. It seemed a little strange to Jamie—they sounded just like her friends when they were having fun.

Jamie peered through the bleachers. Brianna was just getting on the ice, wearing a black and yellow leotard with a black practice skirt and black tights. Her curly black hair was pulled back in a loose pony-tail, with rings of dark curls escaping around her face. She looked very different from the way she usually did on television, when she normally skated with her hair braided into a bun.

Brianna began warming up by stroking* around the ice to gain speed. After a few waltz jumps*, axels, and practice spins, she went through her programs for the exhibition.

Fascinated, Jamie watched as Brianna performed a perfect triple flip jump. *I wonder if my triple flip will ever look as good as that?*

Brianna practiced several other triple jumps, including a double lutz–triple toe loop combination jump. Several times she fell while attempting a jump. It was encouraging for Jamie to see that even Brianna didn't get every jump perfectly in practice. She made mistakes, too.

Yet even when she fell on a jump, it was easy to see why Brianna was a world champion skater. She skated with enormous speed and precision. Jamie was awestruck. Brianna was even better in person than she seemed on television.

I wonder if she'll try her triple axel? Jamie really wanted to see that jump. The triple axel was one of the most difficult jumps in skating. Brianna had landed a triple axel in the world championship, clinching her gold medal performance. Although many of the top male skaters in the world performed that jump, it was rare among women skaters.

Brianna skated backward crossovers*, setting up for an axel. *Maybe this is the triple,* thought Jamie. She watched while Brianna stepped onto a forward edge and leaped from her left skate into the air, making three and a half full rotations before landing on a right backward edge. It was a slightly shaky landing, but a triple axel nonetheless.

Wow, that was so cool! thought Jamie. She hoped she could land a triple axel someday. She wondered if Brianna would try it again since the landing was a little shaky. Jamie looked around, trying to figure out how to get a better view. It was difficult to see from behind the bleachers.

Jamie climbed up higher on the supports underneath the metal bleachers, peering through the seats toward the ice. But she still couldn't see as well as she wanted, so she made another effort to get higher up.

Hanging on the back of the bleachers, she watched in amazement as Brianna performed another triple axel, this one even better than the first. Wrapped up in the performance Jamie took one more step up the metal frame under the bleachers and—CRASH! Jamie came tumbling off the metal bleachers with a noise that echoed all over the building.

Twelve

Everything got quiet. Brianna had stopped skating, and Jamie could scarcely breathe.

"What was that?" yelled Coach Barnes from the other side of the rink. From where Jamie lay in a muddled heap, she could hear footsteps coming toward her.

Oh, no, I'm in big trouble now! she realized. She sat up, trying to decide if she was okay after her fall.

Coach Barnes was angry. Jamie could see it in her face before she said a word. "Jamie Summers, what are you doing here?"

Jamie searched for an excuse while she scrambled to her feet. "Um, I'm always here in the afternoons—for practice."

Coach Barnes didn't buy it. "Jamie, you knew this afternoon's practice was canceled and that Brianna's practice was off-limits. Do you think you are above all the rules?"

"But—" began Jamie.

"I don't want to hear any excuses, Jamie. I am going to call your mother right now. And Coach Grischenko will hear about it, too!"

Jamie didn't know what to say. Coach Barnes was usually so nice. She had never seen her so angry.

There was no point in trying to explain. Jamie's arm hurt and she rubbed it. Limping forward, she reached for her skate bag she had stashed underneath the bleachers.

The coach's expression softened as she grew concerned. "Are you all right, Jamie?" she asked in a gentler tone.

"Um, I think so," she answered.

Coach Barnes sighed. "Forgive me. I should have found out if you were okay before I flew off the handle."

"I'm sorry, Coach. I *really, really* wanted to meet Brianna."

"Well, here I am," said Brianna, appearing suddenly from around the bleachers.

Jamie was embarrassed. She had so wanted to impress Brianna. *What must she think of me?* thought Jamie, mortified that her idol had heard the scolding by Coach Barnes. *She must think I'm such an idiot!*

"I guess I'd better be going." Jamie picked up her skate bag and limped toward the door. She didn't want Brianna to know who she was.

"Wait!" said Brianna. "I thought you wanted to meet me!"

Jamie turned around, more embarrassed than ever.

Coach Barnes explained, "Jamie's not supposed to be here. I'll call her mother to come pick her up."

"She's not home," Jamie said meekly.

"What about Mrs. Wells?"

"She went shopping," Jamie said.

"Who's picking you up?"

"I think my mom is," Jamie answered.

"I don't mind if she watches," said Brianna.

Coach Barnes looked Jamie straight in the eyes. "Jamie, since you are already here you may stay. However, when your mother comes we will go together and explain the situation to her. Of course, it will be easier on you if you explain *all* the rules you've broken. Do you understand?"

"Yes, ma'am," Jamie said.

"And your name is Jamie what?" asked Brianna.

"Summers. And I've been dying to meet you for the longest time!"

"Jamie is one of our most promising skaters," added Coach Barnes, much to Jamie's surprise.

"Well, I'm honored to meet you, Jamie. You didn't skip school to come this afternoon, I hope?"

"No," replied Jamie. "I go to a private school, and my schedule is arranged so that I can practice in the afternoons."

"And I'm taking your practice time. I'm sorry."

"Oh, that's okay." Jamie smiled. Brianna was really nice!

"I'd better get back to work," said Brianna, heading back to the ice, "but we can talk afterward. Maybe we could get some hot chocolate, okay?"

"That'd be great!" said Jamie. She quickly forgot all about her bruises.

Coach Barnes sighed. "Jamie, I don't want you to tell the other kids until after the exhibition. Okay?"

Jamie nodded yes.

❅ ❆ ❅ ❆ ❅

Brianna practiced for another ten minutes, and Jamie watched while she went through everything in her performance. She couldn't wait to tell the other girls about getting to meet Brianna—but wait—she promised not to tell! Jamie frowned. *I can't believe I can't even tell anyone I've met her!*

"Ready for some hot chocolate?" asked Brianna when she finished skating. Coach Barnes had gone in the office to make some phone calls, so Jamie had Brianna all to herself for a while.

There were vending machines in the lobby, and Brianna purchased hot chocolate for the two of them. They sat down at a table in the snack bar. Brianna looked at the cup suspiciously. "How's the hot chocolate here?" she asked.

Jamie laughed. "It's hot and it's chocolate—isn't that enough?"

Brianna took a sip. "Hmm, someday I'm going to learn to like coffee!"

Jamie giggled. Brianna seemed like one of her friends—in fact, she seemed nicer than any of her friends.

"Now, Jamie," said Brianna, "tell me about yourself. How long have you been skating?"

"Since I was three. I really love it."

"I heard that you recently won first at the Music City Trophy. That's an important competition!"

Jamie was surprised. "How did you know about that?" she asked.

"Tamara Vasiliev is a friend of mine. She trains at my home rink in Colorado."

"Oh!" Jamie didn't quite know what to say. Maybe Brianna wouldn't like it that she beat her friend.

Brianna didn't seem concerned about that. She asked, "What are your goals for your skating?"

Jamie took a deep breath. "Well, last year I won the novice championship in my region. I got to compete at sectionals, but I didn't skate very well there, so I didn't get to go to nationals. But I'm planning to move up to the junior level this year. I've already got three triple jumps." She paused a moment, then continued. "I'm hoping someday I can be a national and world champion, like you."

Jamie wondered if she had said too much. Would Brianna think she was overconfident?

"That's quite a goal, Jamie. Do you understand what it takes to reach world-class level?"

Jamie nodded, a determined set to her chin. "I think so. I'm willing to do whatever it takes, no matter what. Even though sometimes it's lonely. My mom didn't even make it to the last competition."

"I'm sure she wanted to come, Jamie."

"I guess she did," Jamie said cheering up. "She gave me a gift to take with me."

"What was that?"

"A Bible. But it doesn't help me much."

Brianna put down her hot chocolate and looked hard at Jamie. "You remind me of myself at your age. I was a lot like you, hard-working, focused, and full of dreams."

Jamie smiled. *Cool! Even Brianna thinks I'm just like her.*

Brianna continued. "I thought winning the world championship was more important than anything else. I even had hopes of winning the Olympics someday."

"I'll bet you will," put in Jamie.

Brianna smiled back. "We'll see. But whether I win the Olympics or not, I have a goal that matters more to me."

"More important than winning the Olympics?"

"Yes. You see, when I was about your age skating was my entire life. I didn't do anything else. I didn't even go to school; I had tutors. My only friends were skaters, and we were too competitive to be really close."

Jamie nodded. This story sounded very familiar.

"After I began winning important competitions, I even began skipping church. I wanted God to help me win, but I didn't spend much time praying or reading my Bible. There wasn't time! I had to spend all my time training. One day I realized that although I had won almost everything I wanted I wasn't happy. I felt like something was missing.

"I had become a Christian when I was ten years old. Being a Christian means making a commitment to love and obey Jesus. When skating became more important to me than Jesus, I couldn't be truly happy, even with a gold medal."

"But isn't winning a gold medal awfully important?" asked Jamie. "I mean, you can do more for God if you're a champion."

"That's what I thought," said Brianna. "But what I found out was that if I didn't put God first in my life, it didn't matter if I was a world champion or not."

Jamie thought about that. "But don't you care about winning anymore?"

Brianna laughed. "Well, it would be a lie to say I don't care. But I've learned that if I had a drawer full of gold medals, they wouldn't mean anything without God."

Jamie had a lot to think about, but just then Coach Barnes came back. "Those phone calls took longer than I intended," she said. "I hope you weren't in a hurry, Brianna."

"Oh, no," said Brianna. "Jamie and I have had a nice visit."

"Jamie," warned Coach Barnes, "remember, don't tell the other kids about this until after the exhibition."

"It doesn't matter. They won't believe I met her," said Jamie.

Brianna leaned over the table. "Well, what if you invite some of your friends to come early to the exhibition tomorrow night? I'll be warming up about an hour and a half before the show. I'll have a few minutes afterward to talk to you."

"Really? That'd be so cool!" said Jamie.

"Great!" said Brianna. "Come down to the ice level, and I'll try to watch for you and your friends."

"Thanks!" said Jamie. "They won't believe it!"

"And, Jamie," said Brianna, "don't forget what we talked about. I hope all your dreams come true."

"I'll try to remember," promised Jamie.

Coach Barnes walked Brianna to her car, and Jamie sat alone for a few minutes thinking over what Brianna had said. Brianna was so cool! Even more than Jamie had hoped.

Jamie gathered her things and waited for her mother to come. She couldn't wait until the exhibition tomorrow night. Suddenly, she laughed. She couldn't believe she had forgotten to get Brianna's autograph!

Just then Coach Barnes came back into the rink. "Your mother's here. Let's go."

Jamie swallowed hard. Her mother would be angry. But maybe she wouldn't be grounded too long.

Thirteen

"I can't believe we're really going to meet Brianna Hill in person!" exclaimed Shannon.

It was the night of the exhibition, and the kids had come early to watch the warmup session before the show. The girls sat a few rows back from the ice in the huge arena while Brianna Hill practiced along with several other world-class skaters.

"Did she really invite us?" asked Kristen.

"All of us?" asked Tiffany, who had been allowed to come along.

"Yes," answered Jamie. "She told me I could bring my best friends to the rink to meet her. She promised to talk to us for a few minutes after the warmup, if we would wait here by the ice."

"I didn't really believe you when you told us you were going to meet Brianna in person," confessed Kristen.

"How *did* you get to meet her?" asked Amy.

"It's kinda like the tickets. I couldn't tell you we would meet Brianna until we got here. I can't tell you how I met her until after the exhibition," said Jamie. "But I kinda managed to get myself grounded. I won't be going to the mall or on e-mail for the next month."

"Did you see that?" exclaimed Shannon after Brianna did a spectacular jump. "That was a triple axel!"

"I hope *I* can do a triple axel someday," said Amy.

"I intend to," said Jamie.

"Aahh!" Kristen screamed and began frantically trying to brush something off the back of her neck.

"Kristen, hush!" said Amy insistently. "The skaters on the ice are looking at us!"

Jamie doubled over with laughter, having seen Kevin and Manuel sneak up and drop something down Kristen's back.

"It's just a plastic spider!" said Kevin, coming up from behind them along with Manuel. "You're making such a fuss!"

Kristen turned toward Kevin, her face red with embarrassment and anger. "Kevin!" She turned to her friends, who were trying not to giggle. "You wouldn't think it was so funny if they had put a spider down *your* back!"

"I'm sorry, Kristen," apologized Amy, "but it *was* kind of funny. You should have seen yourself jump."

"Come on, Kristen," said Jamie. "It was just a joke." She turned to Kevin and Manuel. "How many critters did you guys buy at the Tropical Cafe, anyway?"

Manuel grinned mysteriously. "Oh, not too many."

"Yeah," agreed Kevin. "See? We wouldn't mind if you pulled a trick like that on us!"

"Oh, yeah?" asked Kristen, her eyes twinkling with mischief. "We'll see how you like it. Just wait!" She winked at her friends. "When you least expect it!"

"We're so scared!" teased Manuel.

"Hey, Kristen," said Jamie, "I've got an idea." She whispered something in Kristen's ear. Kristen grinned, looking at the boys.

"Can I hear, too?" demanded Tiffany, trying to listen.

"We'll tell you later," said Jamie. "Okay, Tiff?"

Tiffany giggled, satisfied at being included.

"No fair!" protested Kevin. "There are five of you and only two of us!"

"You don't mean you're scared of us girls?" teased Amy.

"Hey, we've been missing the practice!" said Jamie, noticing that some of the skaters had left the ice.

"There's Brianna," said Kristen, pointing to a skater coming toward them in a purple velvet practice dress. Brianna's black hair was braided into a bun, with a few curls around her face. The kids left their seats and went down to meet her.

"Hi, Jamie!" said Brianna, greeting her with a smile.

Jamie grinned self-consciously, noticing the admiration of her friends on hearing Brianna's friendly greeting.

"Brianna, these are my friends," said Jamie proudly, and suddenly she realized that having friends was something very special.

"I'm delighted to meet you," said Brianna graciously. "Are all of you skaters?"

"We all skate at the Ice Palace with Jamie," said Kristen.

"That's great!" said Brianna. "You have a wonderful rink—I really enjoyed skating there the last few days. I'm just sorry I couldn't have spent time with all of you. That's the trouble with having such a busy schedule."

"The last few days?" Jamie asked in amazement.

Brianna smiled. "You're in school in the mornings, too."

"If you were there so long, where did you stay?" asked Amy.

"At Susan's house." Brianna smiled.

"I'll bet you get to meet lots of famous skaters," interrupted Shannon.

"Yes, I do," replied Brianna, "but they're not that much different from you guys."

"Except they've got a ton of gold medals!" said Kevin.

Brianna laughed. "But you know, they all had to start out the same way—they've all fallen thousands of times."

Tiffany couldn't stay in the background for long. "I'm going to win the Olympics when I get bigger!" she said brightly.

"Maybe you will," said Brianna. "Work hard, and do what your coach tells you." She looked over the group. "I'll give Coach Barnes an autographed picture for each of you. I wish I had more time to chat, but I have to get ready for the exhibition."

She turned to Jamie. "Jamie, you're so lucky to have so many good friends. Now, don't forget what we talked about: Put Jesus first in your life and everything else will fall into place." Brianna waved to the group and turned to go.

"Wow!" said Amy, after Brianna had gone. "That was *so* cool! Imagine! We got to meet Brianna Hill in person!"

Kristen agreed. "I knew she was a great skater, but I didn't know she was such a neat person."

Even Kevin seemed impressed. "I kind of thought she'd be stuck-up, but she wasn't."

"I didn't know she was a Christian," said Shannon.

"She said she used to be just like me," said Jamie.

Kevin shook his head. "Oh, no! I can just hear it now—we're going to have to put up with the 'queen' act from Jamie after this!"

"No, listen!" protested Jamie. "It wasn't like that, honest." She paused. "I know I've had kind of a big head lately . . ."

"We hadn't noticed!" said Kevin sarcastically.

"Kevin!" scolded Kristen. "Let Jamie talk!"

"Yeah!" said Tiffany, defending her friend. "You're being mean, Kevin!"

"He's right. I've been a real jerk. I'm sorry. Brianna helped me see that I've been worrying too much about the wrong things. She said she did the same thing, but then she realized that it was more important to follow and serve Jesus than to have a great skating career."

"Uh-oh!" said Kevin, poking Manuel. "I see a sermon coming. Let's go get something to eat!"

"I want something to eat, too," put in Tiffany.

"Ask Mom," said Shannon, pointing to the group of mothers sitting behind them. "She's right there."

"Mom!" yelled Tiffany. "Can I have something to eat?"

"Shhh!" scolded the older girls. "People are looking at us."

"Good!" said Tiffany, smiling and looking around. "I want them to see me. I can't wait 'til they come to watch *me* skate at an exhibition."

"Oh, brother!" complained Shannon. "Talk about the 'queen' act."

Jamie just smiled. It was nice to have friends again.

❋ ❋ ❋ ❋ ❋

The ice show was fantastic. Brianna skated two performances. One program was an energetic routine to Irish music; the other to music from the musical *The Phantom of the Opera.*

There were a number of other champion skaters from all over the world performing programs to every type of music imaginable. When it was over, the girls all agreed that Brianna was the best.

Kevin and Manuel disagreed. "I think the man from Kazakhstan was the best," said Kevin. "Besides, men skaters are better than women skaters."

"And that Italian guy was really funny," added Manuel. "I get bored with all this serious stuff."

"You guys are just prejudiced," said Amy.

"Never mind," Jamie reminded her. "We've got a score to even with these guys, remember?"

"Oh, yeah," said Amy with a grin. "You guys better be careful."

Tiffany giggled.

"You guys won't talk so big!" said Kristen.

❇ ❇ ❇ ❇ ❇

That night after Jamie got home from the exhibition, the first thing she did was get out her Bible. Flipping through it, she found Hebrews 12:1–2, the verses Brianna had mentioned on the autographed picture she had given Jamie.

Jamie read: "So let us run the race that is before us and never give up. We should remove from our lives anything that would get in the way. And we should remove the sin that so easily catches us. Let us look only to Jesus. He is the one who began our faith, and he makes our faith perfect."

Jamie thought about that. It was part of the same verse she had liked earlier. She realized that she had been chasing after the wrong goal. Maybe she did have a chance to win national and world championships. To reach this goal, she knew she would have to work very hard. And she would have to give up many things.

Brianna had helped her understand that there was one thing she couldn't afford to give up—her relationship with God.

Fourteen

"Are you ready to give your report, Jamie?" asked Miss Meyers.

"Yes, ma'am," answered Jamie. She felt good about finishing a major assignment on time.

After reading Brianna's biography, Jamie had realized how important it was for Brianna to do well in school. Jamie decided she needed to work harder on her schoolwork. After all, even a world champion needs an education.

Jamie stood in front of the class and gave her report on the history of figure skating. On the bulletin board in the classroom she had placed several posters of famous skaters performing different skating moves. She had arranged a special display of various articles on a small table. There were a pair of figure skates, a skating costume, a couple of her competition medals, and a picture book about the history of figure skating.

The class seemed very interested, especially when Jamie told them a little about her own competition experience. When she finished, Miss Meyers asked if the class had any questions for Jamie.

"How much do you practice?" asked one girl.

"I usually practice every morning before school and in the afternoon for another couple of hours," answered Jamie. "When I have a big competition, sometimes I also practice in the evening, too."

There was a general murmur, and one boy exclaimed, "I can't imagine working that hard skating! Don't you ever get tired and just goof off like everybody else?"

Jamie thought a moment before she answered. "Well, I do get tired—and sometimes I wish I could goof off. But I know that if I goof off I'll never be able to reach my goals."

"Are you going to go to the Olympics?" asked another girl.

"Someday, I hope!" said Jamie. "But there are a lot of other good skaters." She hesitated before going on. "I used to think that being national champion and going to the Olympics was the most important thing in the world. I still want that, but now I know that I need to take time for other important things—like being a good friend and getting an education." She glanced at Miss Meyers, who smiled. "And serving the Lord," she added shyly.

When Jamie sat down in her seat, Heather leaned over and whispered, "That was a great report! I didn't know skating was so interesting. If I come to the rink sometime, do you think you could help me get started?"

"Sure! Just tell me when!" said Jamie enthusiastically. Then Jamie did something she was sorry she had not done before, but it was kind of scary. She was trying to be more of a friend by taking an interest in her friends' lives. "I'll tell you about skating if you'll tell me about riding horses."

"I'd like that," Heather said.

"Maybe you'd like to come to the rink Saturday."

Heather laughed. "I'm almost never home on Saturdays. I don't just *ride* horses. I compete in equestrian events all over the country."

Jamie was surprised. "Wow, I thought I was the only one who traveled a lot."

"No. I have it worse than you. I have a brother and sometimes one parent goes with him and one goes with me. It's the only way we can both compete."

"Does he ride horses?"

"No. He is a national diving champion."

"Wow."

"Yeah, it's a pretty big honor, but I don't let it go to his head. I've got an idea: Maybe sometime I could go with you to one of your competitions, and then you could go with me to one of mine."

"I'd really like that," Jamie said.

Maybe Westbridge Academy isn't so bad after all. I have a friend. Even Miss Meyers is pretty nice as long as I get my homework done, Jamie thought.

It wasn't easy combining school and her skating training, but Jamie knew she could do it. Getting a tutor might work later, but at least for now Jamie realized that Westbridge was the best place for her. Since her mother had to work such long hours, Jamie knew she would be lonely with only Mrs. Wells for company.

"For tomorrow," said Miss Meyers at the end of class, "read pages three hundred forty-two through three hundred fifty-two, and be prepared to discuss them."

Jamie wrote down the assignment carefully; she didn't want to risk getting behind in her work again.

✤ ✤ ✤ ✤ ✤

Coach Grischenko folded her arms and stood by the boards* while Jamie skated the last of the patterns in the junior field moves requirements. "Very much better," she said when Jamie completed the pattern and skated back to her. "It is good you failed your test last time. It made you work harder. Now you are almost ready."

"The test is next week," said Jamie. "Do you think I'll pass?"

The coach thought for a moment, then nodded. "Yes. I think this time you will pass." Then she smiled, "And you will only be thirteen."

Jamie grinned, feeling victorious. Reading Brianna's biography had made Jamie realize that she shouldn't compare her own progress with the progress of anyone else. Whether Brianna, or Tamara Vasiliev, or anyone else had passed a certain level by a certain age didn't really matter. It was much more important to work hard to be the best she could be.

Nevertheless, Jamie knew she reached her own goal only through hard work and perseverance.

✳ ✳ ✳ ✳ ✳

After practice that morning, Jamie joined her friends in the lobby. Kristen and Amy were taking off their skates, while Shannon was busy doing some last-minute studying for a social studies test. Although Tiffany usually skated in the afternoons, she had come to practice that morning with her sister.

"Kristen, has Kevin gotten off the ice yet?" Jamie asked.

"No, he's still in a lesson with his coach," said Kristen. "Why?"

"I've got the snake!" Jamie grinned and held up a large coiled plastic snake. Then she turned to Tiffany. "Did you do your part?"

Tiffany grinned. "Yes."

Amy and Shannon looked up. "Where's his skate bag?" asked Jamie.

"It's that black one next to the bench over there," said Kristen.

"When he unzips his bag," said Jamie, "he'll find it. This is great. Is he looking yet?"

"Just a minute," said Shannon. "Okay, he's looking this way . . . now!"

Jamie flashed the fake snake briefly toward Kevin. It was important he see it. Then she hurriedly unzipped the skate bag, stuffed in the plastic snake, and zipped the bag closed.

Amy giggled. "This should teach him to tease us with fake spiders!"

"You'd better hurry!" warned Shannon. "He's getting off the ice now."

"Here he comes!" giggled Tiffany.

"Now, act *normal!*" whispered Jamie. "It'll spoil everything if he gets suspicious."

By the time Kevin opened the door and walked into the lobby, Jamie was innocently unlacing her skates, Shannon was studying, and Amy was wiping her blades.

Kristen zipped her skate bag closed and stood up. She said, with a twinkle in her brown eyes, "Kevin, Mom will be here any minute!"

Kevin sauntered over to his skate bag and sat down. "Okay, okay!" he said as he bent over to unlace his skates.

Kristen and Jamie looked at each other and grinned, but no one said anything.

Kevin finished unlacing his first skate and casually reached for his bag. All five girls watched expectantly while he unzipped it. But no snake popped out. They exchanged glances.

"Hey, what's this?" asked Kevin calmly, reaching into the bag. He hauled out the plastic snake, still coiled as if ready to strike. "Cool! A fake snake." He gave the girls a wicked grin. "I wonder who put this in my bag? Obviously, someone who didn't know to wind it up." He stuffed the snake back into the skate bag, laughing at how smart he was. "You girls had better watch out—you never know when a snake might crawl into *your* skate bag!"

Kristen sighed loudly. "Come on, Kevin, Mom's waiting," she said.

Kevin finished taking off his other skate and reached under the bench. He grabbed his sneakers and stuck in a foot. Suddenly, he jumped into the air as he grabbed off his shoe. Then he started hopping around. "Get back, get back. Where'd it go?" he yelled before finding his mark and slapping an extremely large scorpion with his shoe. That didn't kill it. He hit it again and it jumped to the bench. He slapped it again . . . and then he realized the girls were all laughing.

"I guess we just didn't know to wind that snake up," said Jamie.

"Good going, Tiff," said Shannon.

"Oh, maybe I was wrong, Kevin. Maybe Mom's not here yet," said Kristen.

"When you least expect it, Kristen. When you all least expect it," Kevin said before he started to laugh. "Hey, have you guys shown this to Manuel yet?"

"No," said Jamie.

"Well, maybe we should," said Kevin.

Fifteen

It was the morning of the skating test, and Jamie was waiting for her turn to skate her field moves again. This time things were very different.

All her friends were there to cheer her on. In fact, Amy was taking the intermediate test for moves in the field, a test Jamie had passed two years ago. Shannon and Kristen were there to provide moral support for both of them.

Even more important, Jamie's mother had come for this test. She helped Jamie get ready and smiled reassuringly before Jamie went into the arena for the test. It was nice to have her mom there.

Amy's test came first, and Jamie waited with her for her turn to skate. Amy was very nervous, so Jamie tried to keep her mind off the test.

"You'll pass easily," Jamie assured her. "I watched you practicing those moves, and they looked better than mine when I passed that test."

Amy shook her head. "I don't know. I thought I was ready, but now my legs feel like jelly. Skating tests make me more nervous than competitions."

"I feel like that, too," agreed Jamie. "But Coach Grischenko wouldn't have told you to sign up for the test unless she thought you were ready." Jamie realized now how true that was. She wished *she* had listened to the coach before she signed herself up for the test the first time.

"But do you think she taught me everything I need to know?" asked Amy.

"Coach Grischenko is one of the very best," said Jamie firmly. And suddenly she realized that it was true. Jamie would have been ready to take this test months ago if she had only worked hard. Although Emily had been a good coach, she hadn't pushed Jamie to practice field moves the way Coach Grischenko had. She would always miss her old coach, but she knew that Coach Grischenko really was the best coach for her now.

"Amy Pederson," called the test chairman. Coach Grischenko motioned for Amy to get on the ice.

"You'll do great," called Jamie.

Amy's test went well, although the judges asked her to skate one pattern over. In the end, however, she passed, and Jamie congratulated her before she got on the ice to skate her own test.

She looked at Coach Grischenko, who nodded to her. Jamie skated to her starting position for the first pattern. The test chairman motioned for her to begin, and one by one she skated the patterns.

This time Jamie knew she was ready, and her confidence showed. By the time she finished all six patterns, she felt sure she had passed.

Jamie could tell Coach Grischenko was pleased with how she skated. She gave Jamie a rare smile when she stepped off the ice.

"Good job," she said. "You have learned that practice must come before medals."

Jamie hesitated. Would the coach understand all that Jamie had learned? "Brianna taught me something, too. That Jesus has to come first, before winning or passing tests."

Coach Grischenko looked interested. "Hmm. It seems you have learned many good lessons, Jamie." The coach smiled and turned to help another student who was taking a test.

Jamie headed for the lobby to find her mother and her friends. Whether she passed or failed the test, she knew she had done her best.

"It looked like you skated great!" said her mother, giving her a hug. "What did your coach say? Does she think you passed?"

Jamie shrugged. "She didn't say, but I think she was pleased. At least, she didn't look mad like last time!"

"I'll bet you passed," said Kristen. "It didn't look like you made any real mistakes."

When the results came a few minutes later, Jamie found that she had indeed passed her test.

"This calls for a celebration!" said Kristen.

"I'm always ready for any excuse to celebrate!" said Amy. "What could we do?"

Jamie looked at her mother. "I don't know," she said slowly. "I would love to go celebrate with you guys, but my mom and I sort of made plans. I guess you'll have to go without me."

"No way!" said Amy. "It wouldn't be a celebration without you!"

"Maybe we could do something this afternoon instead," suggested Kristen. "Go to the movies or something."

Jamie looked at her mother. Mrs. Summers nodded. "You can call your friends when we get home this afternoon."

"Is that okay?" asked Jamie.

"Sure," said Kristen. "By the way, where are you and your mother going?"

Jamie grinned. "I'm taking her to the Tropical Cafe, of course."

❋ ❋ ❋ ❋ ❋

After going home to shower and change, Jamie and her mother headed to the West End Plaza Mall to have lunch at the Tropical Cafe. Because it was Saturday there was a long line to get in, but they were finally seated at a table near a waterfall. Jamie ordered Tropical Chicken and her mother had the Tropical Chicken Salad.

"Isn't this a great place?" asked Jamie. This was her mother's first time to the restaurant. Since they had moved to Walton, she had been so busy she hadn't even been to the mall—*any* mall!

Mrs. Summers looked around at the tropical plants surrounding them. "It's very interesting," she said, "but I'm not sure what all the fuss is about. I've been hearing about this place since we moved here."

Jamie shrugged. "I don't know. It's just different, I guess."

Her mother smiled. "It's about time I had a chance to just hang out with my daughter. You know, Jamie, I'm really very proud of you."

"Thanks, Mom," said Jamie. "I'm glad I passed the test, too."

Her mother shook her head. "Not just because you passed your test. I'm proud of you because you've been able to face the challenges God has given you. You set your goals, and you've worked to meet them."

Jamie felt a warm glow at her mother's praise. "There's just one thing, Mom. I like living in Walton, and Coach Grischenko is a super coach. Even Westbridge Academy isn't so bad now that I've gotten used to it. But—"

"Yes?" Her mother looked at her curiously.

"Mom, I miss being with you," said Jamie. "We never get to spend time together anymore."

"I miss our time together, too," agreed her mother.

"Are you always going to be this busy?"

"Well, this job is more demanding than my last position," answered her mother. "But after the office is set up, things should get a little easier." She looked sad. "I'm sorry it's been such a difficult change for you."

"That's okay, Mom. I guess it hasn't been easy for you either."

"I can't change the way things are," said her mother. "But we can meet this challenge. Let's make a date to get together every Saturday for lunch. Deal?"

"Deal!" said Jamie. She smiled back at her mother. Nothing would ever be the same, but with the help of the Lord things were sure to get better.

"By the way," began her mother, "I never did get in touch with that piano teacher, but I found someone else."

"Oh," said Jamie, disappointed. "So I guess I'll be starting piano again, huh?"

Her mother grinned. "No. Saxophone!"

Jamie looked quickly to see if her mother was kidding. "Really?"

"If you really want to learn," said her mother.

"Thanks, Mom!" said Jamie, while she dug into her dessert. Things were better already!

✽ ✽ ✽ ✽ ✽

Later that afternoon Jamie found herself at the Dairy Haven with her friends.

"Now that you've passed your field moves test," said Amy, "are you going to take the junior freestyle test?"

"I don't know," said Jamie. "I'll take it when Coach Grischenko says I'm ready."

"I hope she'll let me take my next test soon," said Amy. "I really want to move up to intermediate level this year."

"I don't know if you should—" began Jamie.

"There you go again!" said Amy, sounding annoyed.

Jamie looked shocked. "What did I say wrong?" she asked.

"You think you're so great!" complained Amy. "You don't think any of us could be champions except you."

Jamie finally understood. "I'm sorry, Amy. That isn't what I meant at all."

"Then what did you mean?" asked Kristen.

Jamie thought before she answered. "I was just trying to be helpful. I meant maybe you should test the next time. I didn't mean to hurt your feelings. I always seem to say the wrong thing!"

"Yeah, like telling us what a great skater you are," said Amy.

"I guess I have been doing that, haven't I?" Jamie said softly. "I'm really sorry. I have a bad habit of talking without thinking first, don't I?"

"Yes!" said the other girls.

"I'll try to do better," promised Jamie.

"We'll be glad to help you," said Kristen, smiling.

"Just don't tell us how great you are!" added Shannon.

"We don't care if you're a champion or not," said Kristen. "We just want you to be our friend. Deal?"

"Deal!" said Jamie, as she dug into her ice cream. It was great having friends. Jamie suddenly realized that they were worth much more than a gold medal.